i'm right here

stories
tony rauch

Spout Press
St. Paul, MN

I wish to thank the following for their invaluable help and encouragement in assembling this collection: John Colburn, Kelly Green, Chris Watercott, Michelle Filkins, Jeffrey Little, Margret Rauch, Mark Poier and Dan (Cleo) Noyes. Thanks for listening.

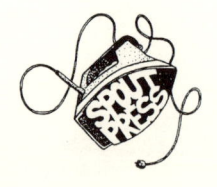

Spout Press
28 West Robie St.
St. Paul, MN 55107

Copyright © 1998 by Spout Press
ISBN 0-9659443-1-X
Edited by John Colburn
Layout by Chris Watercott
Cover design by Tony Rauch
Spout logo Designed by Tony Watercott
First Edition
Manufactured in the United States of America

"Beautiful as a chance encounter of a sewing machine and an umbrella on a dissecting table"

—Lautreamont

"To be free you have to speak a different language. You have to think in another frame of mind. Unity is evil. Only a cowardly idiot would align himself with a unified faction. The outsider presents a threat . . . if you can't convert the outsider, you must destroy the outsider."

—Henry Rollins

Table of Contents

and

1	my second favorite place
6	sometime last week
16	she gave me one of those rare smiles
20	adventure #24
27	dinner with you
31	nine million ways to die
35	I always have the option of killing you
45	and

little fires

61	I'll probably end up writing for tv someday
62	roy's the devil
72	big guys in tight pants
78	adventure #25
84	who's going to sing country western to the urban underprivileged?
89	what I did last night
91	male nude reclining
94	thirty seven

let's wrestle!

107	I was having dinner with scott baio when I saw her again
116	tacoma, 3am
122	blue water, blue sky
138	hated

146	bird in flight
152	car battery sex toy
158	an unusual occurrence
159	an unsightly act of inexpressible horror
160	the boogie man dangling upside down in the rafters of the garage
161	adventure #26
169	dinner one night
170	some more words that remind me of you

1000 stories

173	ecuador
177	her name is radriva pasternak; perhaps you know her
183	the promise
188	all the beautiful women
193	I remember you
195	editorial
197	waiting room
200	two lovers entangled in an unspeakable mess
201	dangle me up the river pajama man
202	1923
203	hullabaloo

and

my second favorite place

My favorite place in Minnesota is the sky. Actually, it's my favorite place just about anywhere. I also like public restrooms, for obvious reasons. But in Minny, it's the sky for me or nothing at all, thank you.

You see, there's this immensely great girl I've just met, and she's like from a totally other planet kind of great. She's just totally boss beyond all recollection, and just dazzling in her own kind of way. And the thing of it is that the sky just gets to couch up there and gaze down on her all day long, while I'm busy doing laundry or working or just getting my ass handed to me in general. And the sky is free to follow her around—as if she owns it, as if it's hers. It gets to breathe down on her and into her life and into her room—and this room has become my second favorite place.

The sky has an open invitation—it can wander in any time—shining in, sliding down the walls, lying on the floor, warming her face, covering her the way I wish I could.

It can hang out with her any time, while I can only wonder how that would be—how her carousel voice and jungle gym words could . . . how her cool stream skin and

i'm right here

warm wind eyes would... how her playground-on-a-summer-afternoon neck should ... how I could somehow believe in these things again.

Though I've never had the pleasure of being invited there, I picture her place—with all of its trapeze artists and Elvis impersonators, all sparkling in their sequined tights and jump suits. I imagine the herds of cats trained to do her laundry. I squint to make out her Cuban revolutionaries—tangoing as only Cuban revolutionaries can. I sense her sheep dogs and genetically engineered dung beetles conferencing over the phone bill, her legion of shoplifting squirrels, her boxing poetry. I recognize her nuclear decontamination crews, dispatched from her processing facilities, sweating in their breathtakingly puffy optic yellow gear, masks fogging, herding the cats and soiled garments.

And what of her rodeos in Joliet? Her roller derby queens from the backwoods of Appalachia? The bliss of ecstasy in her toilet paper? The glory of her truck and tractor pulls? The profundity of her high school guidance counselors? Who's going to speak up for them?

I consider all her other suitors, their mercurial wood chippers, the elastic dreams of their fanciful fishing rods, effervescent gifts to win her over, and all those other things that I can't see—her lullaby voice that could induce labor, her impervious smile that would lay you to slumber.

I'll tell you this—my cloud factories have been working overtime. I had to add a third shift, pussyfooting around the tax laws yet again—and all just to try to impress her. They dispatch mountainous plumes to cover that flat blue—so many clouds I could ride on and signal to her as she lies on her bed or in the grass somewhere, wondering at it all, maybe dreaming, maybe hoping, maybe hoping for someone like me to happen along.

my second favorite place

Maybe if I were lucky, she would picture me, maybe think of me in some small way, and come to realize that all of these clouds, all of these skies, all of these seasons were for us.

I hope I'll see her out there again sometime. Maybe I'll bump into her and strike up a conversation and we'll get together and end up hanging out at my place, a cloud floating over her like a bed, with a squadron of other mattresses floating behind in formation. And I'll impress her with my Tater Tot reheating competency, or with my ability to do laundry, or my aptitude for constructing intricate peanut butter and jelly sandwiches, or with my radically advanced sentence structures.

And she would open up and share her many enigmatic treasures with me—the surreptitious euphoria of her coal-mining gear, the elation of her compliant forklifts, the joy of her irrigation equipment, the epic pleasure in her heavy earth-moving gadgets, the freedom of paradise in her fleeting glimpses, the ephemeral millennium of her falling water hair, the heroic detail of her voluminous collection of spiffy old cement trucks—a veritable history of the cement truck— all operated by her acrobatic tumbling teams, the beautiful tones from her metal shredder, the tranquillity of her misty ambiguous qualities, the anticipation of her tattoo removal doodads, her depressed alcoholic anchormen—leaving the toilet seat up as only depressed alcoholic anchormen can— the eventuality of her amorphous welding crews, the stench of her impending Bigfoots, her apostolic shrine to Siskel and Ebert, the serenity of her evangelical gelatin molds, the enunciation of her wedding cake figurines, the prospects of her eternal Mr. Spock outfits . . .

No lie, Pal, my clunky, uncoordinated nature would compliment these momentary accoutrements. There's no

i'm right here

doubt, Jack—she would add new dimensions to my sandwich making prowess. Surely, Jasper, our strides down the sidewalk on Sunday afternoons would cause minor accidents, if not seizures in small animals.

So many possibilities, so many that I could only be so lucky. You see, if I could only know her, then maybe, just maybe, I could understand the sky—maybe I could somehow have faith in these things again.

I guess I'll always have that sky of hers. It'll always be with me—to reassure me, to whisper proof that such things still sleep somewhere in my heart, that I can always find them there, sitting on old couches smoking cigarettes and telling dirty jokes—to whisper that such things are still possible, that such wonders still exist. I'll appreciate them all, even if from a distance. At least that could be shared with me—those cloudy smiles, those windy promises. And maybe one fine night I may feel her soft touches of wind promising to stay—to find that warmth next to me when I roll over—a heavenly radiant reminder of all the golden calming lullaby grass we might lie in, even if for just a little while.

All those clouds drift by, man. And I'm in my car. At a dumb stoplight. Stuck in traffic. Lost out there. And they're so free. And an old Naked Raygun song comes on—"I live these lives... They just pass me by... Time flies... And I remember..."

The icicles cling to the fire escapes. The fire escapes dangle off the brick of the building. The neon flashes. It all hangs above me. Shadows drop like forgotten pianos. Shadows hang, like broken clocks. Shadows swing, like empty doorways. She lives up there. Her room is up there on the corner, as if in the sky itself. She looms above me. The Lowry

my second favorite place

Hill apartments. Hennepin and Franklin. The liquor stores. The ice cream shops. The rock stars overdosing. And I'm always stuck at that damn light. But she's up in the clouds, floating above me, up where she belongs. Up there with the dance studios. Up there with the blowing golden leaves. Up there in those clouds.

All those Cuban revolutionaries, loyal to the bitter end—who else could you count on, who else could you believe in? All those trapeze artists, swinging for me, liking me for what I am, whatever that could be today. Those depressed alcoholic anchormen, with their supportive nods, somehow filling me, somehow resurrecting my faith. The nobility of all those repentant Watergate conspirators, their conspiratorial smirks, their incorrigible black suits, gardening as only misguided political appointees can. The beautiful melancholy of her massive supercomputers. The devotion of her omniscient librarians, each a few days older than God, each surpassing all conscious knowledge, cleaning the bathroom, deodorizing the hamper...

And, although I can see all of these things, none of them seems to be within my reach. And the day passes. And so many other people wander by. And I still feel that soft whisper of wind inside of me—as if maybe, after all, in some small way, somewhere, there may just be someone else waiting out there.

sometime last week
(*story to send to the* New Yorker)

1.

I recall I had been thinking about it for some time. I had been kicking it around all day, thinking of sitting down and finally writing it all out—that movie script I had been promising myself. It would be a vehicle for Jason Robards, a fine actor and a gentleman—I reasoned. In it he would be a serial killer. Or maybe a game-show host.

Though I'm not very gifted with language, or narrative ability, the story would nevertheless be a real spellbinder. I dream that it gets published, made into a movie, or produced as a play. I dream that somehow it gains some small measure of notoriety or recognition that requires me to give an interview. The interview would be for some local television show, newspaper, or obscure arts journal. They'll want to photograph me in front of a bookcase, like they always seem to do in these instances—you know the ones with all the old, heavy, dusty, moldy, hardcover books no one ever reads. But I'll refuse and insist upon having my portrait photographed in front of a tall bookcase lined from floor to ceiling with hams.

sometime last week

I picture myself sitting there, blinking, reflectively staring off into the distance and saying things like: "Somehow, ham really inspires me." In time I'll take to wearing clothing made of ham—because that's the type of thing that a "real" artist would do.

And when they ask me the inevitable "What's next" questions, I'll state flatly, "To become the commissioner of the National Basketball Association, where I'll institute some new rules—like the Amish rule, for example, that all players must grow a league standard Amish type beard. Also, all uniforms will be made of rotting lettuce fermented in warehouses in small towns in the Southwest."

I'll be soft-spoken and polite, but go off on tangents, the way "thoughtful" people do: "People are impressed with my wrestling competency, though it is not widely known I possess such aptitude. I am an expert, as much as one can be, at what is referred to as 'submission' style wrestling. My specialty is the infamously torturous, yet cowardly, 'groin kick.' It is revered, and banned in many states—even several down South.

"I trained in the Orient, where I perfected other such cowardly maneuvers as the 'Adam's apple pinch' and the 'stomach grab' and the 'spread vicious rumors behind their back' move. I tested my mettle in their 'triangle' matches— three sweaty guys in lycra tights in a ring smeared with butter with a starved 350-pound hog, a boa constrictor, an embittered artist, some cockroaches, and a dozen tapeworms."

I'll pause dramatically and continue on as thoughtfully as possible. "Spectators are then allowed, through the course of the match, to hurl things at the combatants. But they are restricted to throwing only things which they have smuggled into the building. So when such a contest is staged, it is of special interest to lurk around in front of the arena beforehand and make note of the items being snuck in: golf balls, old batteries, various produce, small barnyard animals, flügelhorns, old tube-style vacuum cleaners, toasters, blenders, and the like."

2.

I begin rummaging in a drawer for a pen and paper with which to initiate the manuscript. The television is on for some measure of background effect and ambience. A low budget, minor league professional wrestling program is on an obscure cable access channel—one of the really high number stations on the dial. This program is from Texas—a bonus, as I gain most of my inspiration from such artifacts.

The so-called "Macho Man" Randy Savage is engaged in a gentle, philosophical discussion with one of the announcers. Not a man of idle words, he begins flailing his limbs and pointing menacingly into the camera, ranting passionately about how "the door of opportunity is wide open" and that "you can only bust through if you are ready, if you see it, feel it, and recognize it."

"Sound advice," affirms the so-called "Mean Gene" Okerlund, the hearty announcer, always quick with a smile and supportive, yet professional to the bone. "You sound like a true Dale Carnegie disciple," he adds. Randy stands frozen in thought, sweating profusely, his head darting like a hummingbird. He finally says quietly, incredulously, "Well, I never wrestled Dale Carnegie."

The action swiftly switches to the ring where Lt. James Earl of the "Highway Patrolmen" tag team is working on the back of the neck of one of the "Super Assassins" with the big elbow and what looks to be a cheese grater from the stadium commissary. I make a mental note: To shore up my credibility in the community I must hurry down to the "Men's Wearhouse" and acquire a sports jacket just like Mean Gene's, and promptly. I make another mental note: To shriek at high volume, in a southern tone, as I enter: *"It's butt-whuppin' time!"*

I settle into the couch, one of my roommate's oft rebuffed articles laying before me on the coffee table like a sudden island. It has been rejected by every major wrestling fan magazine, even the ones from Mexico. I suggested a change of title to enhance its tone, as perhaps "Get a Life You Smelly, Hairy, Uneducated Hillbilly Weirdoes" may appear, at first glance, just a tad too negative.

It's actually a very positive declaration on sportsmanship and camaraderie, just as his "Take off those masks. What are you trying to hide, you yellow-bellied, slack-jawed cowards?" was a succinct plea to the industry for pride and self-esteem. I made a suggestion for him to try an angle which isn't so heavy in tone and disenchanting.

I haven't seen him all day. He is probably out on his moped, guzzling cough medicine and kicking the side mirrors off cars, a favorite sport of his which he has titled "Leaving something behind." He likes to get an early start. He warms up by kicking over garbage cans, spilling their contents as he passes. He thinks it's "cool."

I've been distracted like this all day, tweaked in fact, in that spazzed-out way after surviving that nightmare from the previous evening. It started out as a fantastic erotic dream—as usual the Gabor sisters were Roller Derby queens from the early 1960s—all decked out in flashy, malodorous lycra leotards, gritting their teeth and swinging their arms around in a menacing windmill style, zipping around like a wildcat oil strike. Hell on wheels. Fucking tornadoes.

i'm right here

Their thick blue mascara and taut, tight, plutonium-dense beehive hairdos gave me that sexy/claustrophobic, fear-of-flying/bus driver/lunchroom lady feeling that tingled up from my groin as if bubbling up from my very soul, as if right out of the murky depths of the "pledge of allegiance" itself.

Yes, oh yes, the Gabor sisters in all their glory, in all their cold-war portrait-of-mayhem and total-pandemonium splendor. I am woozy from the nostalgia.

They started by swinging me around by the arm—"Irish whip" style. And before I knew what hit me they were slipping off their go-go boot roller skates and peeling down their sweaty lycra. I began to climax, again, as usual. Only this time, I don't know, they musta blew a circuit in my system because I couldn't stop, and gradually filled my bedroom. Ecstatically, I drowned in my own throbbing pleasures—eyes rolled back, lids blinking, body twitching.

It ended with the terror of my mom finding my lifeless, though still hard, body. All the love juice had eventually drained out of the room, much of it soaking into the carpet to drip through the floorboards and onto the kitchen table below, and just as she was setting it for breakfast the next morning.

Zsa Zsa had scrambled eggs. Eva enjoyed French toast on my father's lap while my mother mopped.

3.

I really should get to my random calls. That's been a big thing around here lately—just dialing randomly and leaving a little message from right out of the blue. Something in a soft whisper. Something like: "Yoooouuu smmeeelll" or "I'm gonna fucking kill you tonight" or "Lather me up, big boy." I reach for the phone. We have over three dozen phones hooked up—most of them stolen from hospitals, hotels, schools, places like that. My roommate calls it "knap-sacking." In fact, there are maybe three things in here total that aren't stolen, and you're one of 'em. It's not that we collect phones or anything; it's a convenience thing. We just can't stand being within reach of at least one phone, if not four or five.

I hold the receiver to my ear. But I can't think of anything profound. I put the phone down. That dream got me to thinking about this crummy little shit hole and about my crummy little room here. It's one of those either way-too-hot or way-too-cold rooms. Stuffy and flat and faded and matted and moldy and reeking of last week's beer, not nearly enough room for *either* of the Gabor sisters to whirl me around in.

My lease renewal has been due for over a month, but I can't decide if I should stay or not, or I haven't really thought about it. Not much anyhow. It gets me to thinking about how time creeps by infinitesimally slowly—tiptoes by imperceptibly—like Zsa Zsa gripping a midget wrestler in a "Boston crab" (yet another sexy submission hold in her enviably shrewd arsenal) and of those randy alley cats waking me from that dream with their symphonic lovemaking, just below my curious, open window.

I hear the past months lapping at my shores. The thought of another year here slowly bringing it all back. Nothing much. Or nothing much different anyway. I think I should sit down and figure things out. Or at least I think I should start.

I settle in with my roommate's pad and pen and begin a list of "good things" and "bad things" from the past year.

i'm right here

Bad: bad jobs, bad pay, bad girlfriend, bad friends, bad apartment, bad rash, no girl, no friends, no respect, the same $3 in my pockets that I've had for the past four years... Well, at least I'm not bogged down with any responsibilities.

Just as I was touching pen to paper for the "good" side you happened to ring my buzzer. You coaxed me out. And just as I was going to outline it—put it all down, write it all up, script it all out. Jason Robards in a stellar powder-blue leisure suit. But you stopped over. And you coaxed me. And we went out and got really shit-faced instead.

4.

On the way to that dark, pathetic little bar we toked up a big duber in your Gremlin. Faded an early '70s baby blue and speckled with rust, you called it "the sky." I asked you, once when we were gettin' wide in it on a sunny Sunday afternoon once. I asked you once what your favorite thing was. And you paused for a moment and then cleared your throat and said, "The sky."

I was really fucking baked by the time we finally arrived. The place was preposterously dark. Absurdly dark and dank and just really really cave like. Just like always. Just the way I like it.

We settled in and after a few I noticed an old girlfriend perched several tables away. The tables were really high, the ones with the tall bar stools. So she was sitting up where I could see everything; where I could see her tight red dress clinging to her, gripping her in its fist. And she was leaning this way and that, and swaying where I could get a good long gander at her everything, at her every possibility.

sometime last week

I put on my macho face, got all serious and macho and aggressive. I had been thinking about her a lot lately. I had, in fact, planned on calling her, maybe even that very night if I got up the old ambition.

I pictured her sauntering over to this table, swinging from side to side, willowing through the dark crowd. She'd put her arm around me and lean in, rubbing against me and whispering some little tragically romantic and sexy thing, something like "Lather me up, big boy."

I wanted to let her know how I felt and how I had missed her greatly, but I didn't know how to tell her. I pictured myself sitting next to her. And all was quiet. All her friends were far far away. And there were no other guys around to butt in and ruin things. And I was just sitting there with her. And everything was all smooth and quiet and dark. And she was paying every last bit of attention to me. And I was lavishing all this attention back on her, uttering smooth things to her night, whispering things like: "I promised myself I wouldn't rush into anything, I promised myself I'd be patient and calm—for once in my life—and not get serious too soon, not to over extend myself or cheat us out of anything. I promised myself I wouldn't even kiss you. I wouldn't even try to kiss you, not even ever so lightly. But looking at you now, here in the brightness of this candle, in this world of a halo of a candle, a tidal wave of doubts and dreams and hope being washed upon the beaches of your lips and your eyes—it's all I can think about, as if it were all I could ever think about. And it's all I want to do, as if it were all I ever wanted to do."

I was gazing at her through the crowd. I wasn't staring really, just gazing as if in a daydream. And suddenly I caught her eye. She noticed me. She slid down from that lanky stool and took a step toward me. But then you said

i'm right here

something really funny and then laid down this hellacious lion's roar of a fart, and just as she looked over at me, I was laughing so hard from the liquor and the beer and the weed and the fart that beer began bubbling and gushing from my nose.

It's the last thing I can remember. They say vomit began shooting out of my nose just after that, but I'm not sure if that's really accurate. Could be. The beer coming out was the last thing I remember before the bouncers dragged me by the ankles, face down, through the bar and slung me into the back alley. Apparently I had lost consciousness. I came to in a pool of smells I was ashamed of, in a pool of what appeared to be my own vomit. Or, well, somebody's vomit. As an extra bonus, I had pissed myself. I found out much later, at home in fact, that at some point, I had indeed shit myself to boot.

My clothes reeked and she was gone. I looked around, but she was nowhere to be found. You drove me home. I yacked in your car and hoarked on the sidewalk as you dragged me in. While you dragged me upstairs I ruped down my shirt and pissed myself again, yet another warm ritual I was getting to become quite friendly with. Then, if I got the chronology right, I passed out on the couch, in front of the TV.

I came to on the floor the next morning with a mouthful of matted, dirty, orange shag rug. The TV flickered, washing down on me a stark black and white, illuminating a now-standard custom in my culture.

Black Jack Lanza had Doctor X in a paralyzing headlock. But the good Doctor deftly slipped past him and dropped into a devastating step-over toehold. Mad Dog Vachon pulled a hopeful, spiffy garlic press from the damp depths of his trunks. He gripped it tightly and reached to apply it to Vern Gagne's nose.

sometime last week

Later, when I checked, there was a message on my answering machine. Some girl with a silky, deep, husky, comforting voice. She whispered her random advice: "Never give up hope." I sat on the floor, in the dark, and listened to it all day long.

she gave me one of those rare smiles

Tokyo trembled as I spread peanut butter on my bread, as if my peanut butter controlled seismic zones. And suddenly, like a glass falling off a table, she was right there. She gave me one of those rare smiles, the kind I hardly ever get from girls anymore. The kind that says, "Gosh, I think I might actually like talking to you."

A guy went into a bar across the street, with an old stuffed duck tucked under his arm. I watched him curiously out of the window, through her smile. And right then, I hopelessly pictured a time very soon when she would have to walk away, and I would have to think of something to say to draw her back to me, but I wouldn't be able to form the words to say some ancient version of "Hey, I enjoyed talking to you. Would you like to do it again sometime?" And I would just be left standing there as she walked away.

"Emmm, this chicken is good."
"You mean I'm fat!"
"I think I'll watch the game."
"You mean I'm fat!"
"Nobody ever listens to me. . . and I can't ever get anything done."
"You mean I'm fat!"

Conversations circled like spring robins and we sat together at the restaurant and talked about work. I couldn't

she gave me one of those rare smiles

believe my luck. I was stunned. There I was—next to her, like . . . like . . . like a statue of hope.

"No Christmas bonuses this year, huh? Hhhmmm, I'll have to adjust my pajama budget accordingly."

"Meow meow meow," she began talking a magic kitty talk, as if she were the queen of all the kitties. "Meow meow meow."

"Oh," I replied, "oven mitts, wow."

"Meow meow meow meow?"

"A surprise party for me? Hell yeah, that'd be great, I'd love it."

"Meow meow meow meow meow?"

"Well, that's getting a little personal now, don't you think?"

"Meow meow meow meow meow meow meow meow meow meow meow meow . . ."

"Hey, if you're going to speak with me, please . . . please try to keep a civil tongue in your mouth."

"Meow."

"Yes well, that's perfectly understandable—I'm frightened of beards too."

"Meow meow meow meow meow meow meow meow meow meow meow meow. Meow meow meow meow meow meow meow meow meow meow meow meow, meow meow meow meow meow meow, meow meow meow meow meow meow meow meow. Meow meow meow meow meow meow meow meow meow (she was talking a blue streak now) meow meow meow meow meow meow meow meow meow meow meow meow meow meow meow meow meow meow meow meow meow meow meow meow meow meow meow meow meow meow meow meow meow meow meow meow meow meow meow meow meow meow meow."

"No, I don't think it's unusual to want to dress up as Abe Lincoln, I guess. I suppose in many places it's considered

i'm right here

quite socially acceptable—in his hometown, perhaps. On his birthday, maybe. . . . Say, how's your little sister doing?"
"Meow meow."
"Wow, she's dating already?"
"Meow."
"Five boyfriends. Gee whiz, what a little heart breaker."

I remember she gave me one of those rare smiles, like an enormous battle scene. The kind that says "You're a big kitty." The kind that says "Lets go hunt us some gators." The kind that says she wants me to be something that . . . something that I'm not. The kind that has the entire world wrapped up in it. The kind that makes me feel like the luckiest person on earth.

And after that biblical smile unfolded like a millennium of summer mornings, she just sat there and stared down at her feet for a while. I could live forever there in that moment, sitting there next to her, my mind going blank, my hands shaking, my mouth dry, scared stupid in awe like always. I could live there forever. I could remember how good that felt. I could remember how terrible that felt.

I felt so lucky to be just sitting there, even if for just those few golden moments. And I watched those moments flicker through me, flowing through my hands like sunshine.

In that restaurant, that landmark, that holy place, I watched her tenderly carve a poem into her pork chop:

> you poignant, profound
> you monkey-lovin' goober
> at last, you are you

And I spread a poem with my peanut butter

she gave me one of those rare smiles

> you pitch that smile
> a tent in my heart
> a place for you to sleep

. . . and Tokyo trembled, jiggling and swaying back and forth. But they were out of beer. So I put down my fork, and began trashing the place, throwing things and tipping things over—dishes and plates and tables and chairs. I was nervous, after all. I wanted to impress her, after all. I wanted everything to be perfect for her (me being the introspective and complicated man that I am). And she just laughed and laughed as they dragged me out, kicking and wiggling, and finally tossed me, in one fluid poetic motion, into a snowbank. And as she gathered her stuff, putting on her adorable little blue jacket and wrapping herself in that beautiful scarf and hitching up that purse, she turned to watch me out the window, standing on the sidewalk with my back to her, urinating into that snowbank.

I wrote in the snow with my own pee. And I could feel her smiling a broad smile of approval and giggling as I slowly moved my hips back and forth. Then I zipped up, walked down the sidewalk, and turned my head to watch her breath gently fogging, blooming in the crisp air like angels.

I could feel her stepping from the restaurant. I could feel her standing, looking down. I could feel her smiling there, just a little smile, hitching up that purse, adjusting that knitted cap . . .

> now she drifts away
> without knowing how I feel
> if she ever will

I remember, one time, she gave me one of those rare smiles. I remember.

adventure #24

"Maybe go out on a love binge," I answered. "I'm a binge lover myself." The lazy, apathetic light hung itself over me like lace—grainy with dust and cynicism, leaving Jean-Claude in the dense expanse of breathing, pulsating darkness. His face faded in and out of recognition. I didn't know it then but he wasn't the structural expert they claimed. Later that night, my crew would come to rat him out for what he was: one of the most cunningly vulturous undercover men in the business.

"What do you plan on doing?" I returned his question concerning the impending, steamrolling weekend. There was a long pause as its shadow loomed over us. Out of the corner of my eye I could see waves of gray light wash him in and out of view. His head moved in and out of that emaciated light. He shrugged and tilted his head from behind his drafting board. "Oh, I don't know," he began in his dry, raspy voice, just chewing it over out loud. He never did answer, though.

We were finishing the drawings for the government, a prototype building, a real hush-hush deal that just landed in our laps right out of nowhere. It was for the Air Force they told us, an international, prototype storage facility. That's all

adventure #24

we knew, other than the specifications, which were relayed to us in code, sent by specially trained Cat Trout, many losing their lives as decoys—to bears and such. The ones that did make it were delicious. After we caught and fried them, we sat around the fire, our waders hanging from the branches. We smoked our cigarettes and told stories of lost loves and close calls. Unfortunately, the radio crackled the coded message too late. Just as we were rinsing the china in the Cat Trout stream, Davis walked down to us and whispered how we were supposed to *release* the Cat Trout that made it, so the other side's Cat Trout wouldn't get wise. Davis and I ran up the bank, back to the fire, desperately trying to account for all the hides we nabbed, about twelve in all, but could only come up with eleven. I looked around. They were big suckers, gutted cleanly, the size of sleeping bags. As I lined them up to be photographed, Kenny, always the clown, climbed inside one. He stepped into it, pulled it on and hopped around like a ridiculous fool. "Look everybody, I'm a Cat Trout!" he shouted with a big, silly grin as he jumped, kicking up a cloud of campsite dust.

Davis was drawing somewhere out in the darkness. He liked it that way, out on his own, in the tall grass, the bugs jumping around his ankles in the clearing, under the lonely moon he conjured with his slow dance.

It was late at night, really late, like I-don't-even-know-what-time-it-is late. I could hear Davis's parallel rule sliding up and down and the click-clack of his scale and triangle echoing in the meadow. "Whaddaya s'pose these buildin's are fer?" he shouted out of the darkness. "Secret research," I speculated without looking up from my table. "Ellllvis research," Spider, the red-neck, offered from the night as some crickets chirped. "An Elvis cloning center."

i'm right here

"To house the Norwegian Vikings brought back through time," Davis added, as an owl wooed. "Between the Elvises and the Hitlers they've been keeping us pretty busy, eh Claude?" I asked in an attempt to keep him in the group. I looked over at him, but didn't get his attention.

"Aliens, man. Aliens," Kenny called out.

At this Jean-Claude looked up, a sinister brooding look under his forehead. They told me before he got here that he had just lost his father. You know you're a man when your father goes, so I didn't press the point. He just stared over in the direction of Kenny. "Aliens," Kenny said again. "They're buildings to house all the aliens."

Eventually the night's tide pulled us down deeper into itself, and we began to doze off.

Hopper woke me in the dim mist of early morning. I was hunched over my drafting table, my head in my arms. Hopper told me he had noticed the #3 exhibiting note-taking tendencies. I thanked him as I rubbed my eyes, as if it were my responsibility. He handed me a little "while you were out" message that was written on a thin slip of pink paper. It said, "The chameleon will leave a package for you in the second garbage can in the alley behind Leopard's house. The package will be in a brown bag with an 'X' marked on it with a laundry marker." He handed me another message as I yawned. I thanked him, and he turned and walked down to the stream.

I slid off my drafting stool and rubbed my hair, reading the message in the cold, weak light. It said something about some copper tubing, Elmer's glue, some glitter, and a large bronze camel. I couldn't really read it, the writing was so bad, but I got a vague recollection of wanting to go to the Piggly-Wiggly to buy all the children there glitter and glue, maybe some construction paper, if they had any.

22

adventure #24

     I looked up as I walked and saw the #3 resting on a large rock down the stream a ways. He was hunched over a notebook. He was down there slammin' them words together again—slappin' em, stackin' em, stackin' em up down by the river there. How high can he stack them? I don't know. The long, gold grass waved about him in the loud, gusty wind. I stopped to listen to it, to enjoy it, and as I listened I picked out a vague commotion that faded in and out of the morning air. I turned to the commotion rising up over the golden grass of the ridge. I put my hand over my forehead as they were coming through the trees, out of the rising light.
     It was the gang, and they were dragging Jean-Claude. I thought he was maybe drunk, and they were just returning him from the cusp of a long night of festivities. But Jean-Claude had never been seen exhibiting festive tendencies before.
     They dragged him through the dust and brittle underbrush and dropped him at my feet. He was wearing a cold, mean stare. "He's one of them," huffed Spider. Hopper hopped up and down. "He's one of them, Oh Goddy he's one of them." He hopped around in a circle, slapping the top of his head with his palm, slap slap slap, and crying like a stuck pig until Davis slapped him, knocking him into the sand with a puff of dust. "He's one of them, man," Spider said, his voice quivering as if in a thirty below wind. I rubbed my face, mushing it around, and exhaled the last few days. "I picked a fight with him, you know, 'cause that's what I sort of do, on my free time." Spider was right as rain there, that's why he was a redneck. "Yeah, yeah," he said excitedly. "I was pokin' my nose in his business," he explained pointing his finger into my face. "An ya know, he didn't really respond like most people 'round these parts do." He was shaking his head a little,

i'm right here

looking at me out of the corner of his eye. "So we all worked on 'em 'til we found these." He pulled some papers from his back pocket and whipped them around to me. I held them, surveying them cautiously, passing one on top of the other. The paper was thick and heavy and stiff. And Spider was right, they found his papers on him.

"He's an alien!" squealed Kenny in a panic as he reached down behind himself, drawing up a solid shaft of smooth driftwood from the rocks. Swinging it above his head in one graceful motion, he thumped it down into Jean-Claude's midsection with a hearty "whump." His body curled around Kenny's whack stick. All the air that had ever been in him rushed out his mouth. He stayed that way, curled with a surprised, whistling pucker on his face, his eyes as big as frying eggs.

Kenny dropped the stick and bolted. He took off in a frenzy, kicking up dirt as he scrambled up the ridge to the fire. He came back our way seconds later, sliding back down the ditch on one of the Cat Trout hides. He slid on the long grass—zipping right by us with a determined, presidential look—as if a sled on snow, finally skidding to a halt in the sand ten feet upstream.

We watched with puzzled looks as he climbed out of the slippery hide and situated it in the water, carefully stepped into it and rode the current past us. "I'llllll gooooo fooooor heeellllp!" he cried as he bounced past our big, mouth-open faces.

I knew we couldn't use the radio because another double agent might pick up the call, and there was no telling what Kenny would do in his excited, reactionary state. "I'll get someone," I exhaled, as I turned and started for the gas station up the road.

adventure #24

I should never have left them alone.

Later, I found out they had dragged Jean-Claude down to the stream and applied their own sort of pressure vis-á-vis the water and large smooth stones, discovering that we were right all along. The buildings *were* for the Elvises, little ones and big ones, and for all the Norwegian Vikings—angry, confused Norwegian Vikings—and for the aliens, benevolent aliens—shifty, sneaky, aliens, disinterested, apathetic aliens—all kinds.

Davis met me at the hospital. I had called an emergency helicopter which went out and brought everyone back. Jean-Claude was in surgery, with a dozen federal agents outside the door as we huddled about what to do with the building plans. "Someone's going to build it anyways, so why not get in on the ground floor of this Elvis research?" Davis offered. "But is it moral to bring Norwegian Vikings back through time?" argued Hopper. "And what about the aliens?" pleaded Spider. "Where they gonna live? I don't want no aliens in my neighborhood. They're funny-lookin', and they probably smell." I had to admit this did make tantalizing redneck logic. I mean, what about the aliens? Besides all the abductions and cattle mutilations, they've pretty much kept to themselves.

We stood in the hospital corridor, debating, with the rolled-up drawings tucked under our arms, the federal agents badgering us with questions. We reevaluated our collective unresolved feelings for Elvis, snipping them out and pasting them neatly in a scrapbook we got down at the nice little gift shop in the lobby run by a stocky lady named Dotty. Would we have him back and all? We asked Dotty. Would we pick him up at the bus station? Would we drive him to the impound lot if he got towed? Even if he was behaving foolishly? Yer damn straight we would.

i'm right here

Let's do it, we agreed. Let's do it for the aliens. Let's do it for the Vikings. Whether they want to be here or not, they deserve a hospitable stay. Let's do it for Elvis, *all* the Elvises. Who's to say such technology won't benefit humanity. Think of the Christmas specials. Who knows, if all goes right we could have crooning Elvis lawyers and darkly cool Elvis baby-sitters roaming our cities, filling up the unemployment office, clogging the violations bureau, driving around aimlessly with shiftless teenagers at all hours of the night, chaperoning beach parties, racing stock cars, running for public office, taking the postal exam. Hell, I'd help him study, you bet I would, try and stop me.

Just as our idealistic enthusiasm was budding into something unexpectedly beautiful, the federal agents knocked us down, racing Jean-Claude down the hall on a gurney, their smooth black hair waving, their sunglasses and black suits shining on the clean yellow ceramic tile of the hall, their features looking just a little too similar to you-know-who.

It seemed Kenny was one of them, too. His agents intercepted my call to the authorities from the gas station. We led them right to Jean-Claude, who had recorded our plans on microfilm as we slept. Their doctors patched him, then whisked him up to the roof and off in a helicopter—off to one of their tremendously exotic hideouts, to tinker with the coveted Elvis technology, to live new adventures, to relax with their exotic toys, their exotic weapons, and their exotic women.

dinner with you

    I was thinking about you the other night. I was just sitting around after work and dreaming of you, dreaming about what you were doing at that moment and about what you were like, wishing I knew more of you, wishing I had a chance to talk to you, wishing you were interested in me, dreaming you were here, dreaming that I knew you.

    I was making a sandwich for myself and thinking about sustenance, such a complex notion. And I was thinking about all the things a guy needs and about all the dreams I had when I was a kid. I was sort of lazily taking inventory, thinking about all the dreams I had built on all the beaches all over the world when I was a kid. I had left them all out there, waiting out there like promises, waiting for me to return and inhabit them—with someone like you.

    But it just got to be too much to take—the empty room staring at me expectantly, like a drained lake, like a black fog—the room without you, the room without you—I couldn't take another dinner alone. I had to get out of there, find you wandering out there somewhere. I had to get up and get out, do something, stir up some activity, fold time and space to drag you to me, as if pulling you on a rug. I had to do something to start to get to know you. I had to do something to start that rusty machine in motion. I had to do something

i'm right here

mechanical. I had to do something. I had to do something. So I threw that sandwich away, that one I was practicing on to impress you with. I hopped on my bike hoping hoping hoping to see you, hoping to draw you to me, to drag you back from beyond, hoping it would pull you to me like a gravity machine, hoping to run into you out there in your city, maybe walk with you for a block or two on one of your sidewalks so you could maybe get to know me a little. We could walk for a while and when it was time to say good-bye maybe I could find it somewhere within me to tell you how nice it was to talk to you. And maybe I could somehow operate that machine and somehow command it to ask if you wanted to have lunch sometime, maybe go out for a beer or have some coffee or go for a walk down by the river or maybe sit down and have some dinner together.

It was kind of funny in a sad way, that I've hoped so long now that I could actually close my eyes and see you there, just beyond my fingers, so solid and complete, as if a piece of furniture that I knew well, as if one from my childhood, waiting jealously for me to return from some beach far off in another distant room of the world.

It's gotten so that I feel you in that living room, in all your shallow, shadowy, dreamy angelic clouds—ten skies of clouds—playing with the furniture, picking it up and moving it about like a child, with your warm, flavorful hands rearranging my dreams. I search for you on sidewalks, in lawns, and on steps and porches, like a spy. Searching as if you'd been inside me all my life, just sleeping there in a soft pair of my old pajamas.

After about an hour and a half I decided to give up the search. I started back for home as it was growing dark and colder, with the night's eyes peering over the trees, looking for us.

dinner with you

I stopped by a burger joint and got a bag of grease—a burger and fries to have for supper when I got home. On the way back, all cold and sweaty and alone and scared and feeling bad and mad and hungry and shaky and tired and sad and weak and frustrated and cursing everything that went by—trees and dogs and other guys with their girlfriends and all the places you hang out so far from me and all the other guys you see and God and the day I was born and just then I hit this tremendous pothole and I heard this shhhhiiiffffft sound like something had rattled loose and fallen off the bike. As I glided down the oil-stained and broken-glass-freckled gutter, I slowed and bent down to investigate each side of my bike to make sure it was all there.

  I held the grease-soaked bag in a fist wrapped around the handle bars and noticed after I started up again down the block that the bag was just flapping there in my hand like a sad, flat glove. Its bottom was ripped out under the weight of the soggy grease.

  I turned and cursed my way back up the block to the intersection where that pothole had been resting. When I got back there, I found my french fries spilled in the pothole, as if trying to escape from a large salad bowl. The burger was a few feet away, stampeding out of its soggy wrapper. It sat folded over on itself, slouching inside-out, crawling out of the tissue onto the street like an awakening child from a soft blanket.

  I laid my bike down against the curb and then joined it, sitting down in frustrated anger and began scooping up the burger and setting it on what was left of the bag. The bun was flat as a paper plate and the burger shredded, like the carcass of a small animal on the side of a hot, lonely, forgotten road.

  I sat there on the curb looking down on it all. There wasn't much I could do with it. In my professional estimation,

i'm right here

it was simply beyond repair, so I began eating, picking the ground-up meat and strands of bread, indistinguishable from one another, and began lifting them between my fingers, raising the street up to my mouth and chewing, with sand and pebbles crunching and grinding against my teeth, gladly swallowing tar and gravel and gnawing more sand.

I sat at your dinner table, with large oil stains for place mats, and plates of grease and gas spots, and sticks and leaves for tableware. And suddenly I noticed you coming up the block—you were walking with your friend Maureen and that other girl that I don't like as I chewed spitefully.

You were wearing that heartbreakingly tight shirt with the really low-cut neck and all those breathtaking colors screaming by in stripes, a thousand colors cruising along at a thousand miles per hour. And you had on those beautiful faded black jeans that reminded me of the nice roads that would lead me back to all those beaches where everything was warm and pleasant and calm.

You stepped off the sidewalk from across the street and landed on your table. And you were coming right this way, and I was just sitting there before you on the ground—in the sand—eating dirt.

nine million ways to die

The women at the bowling alley are ignoring me. It makes me feel light. Naked. Invisible. Me being thin-skinned and all.
    The girls won't talk to me. Nobody likes me. I feel lonely. I feel ashamed. It's as simple as that. I never knew how alone a person could get. It is the worst kind of pain. It feels like I'm dying a million times over, each death slower than the last. It is the worst thing to do to someone—to ignore them.
    I sigh and gaze longingly at the girls strenuously exercising on a vast, empty beach in their bacon bikinis on the television. An evangelist for Exxon struts contemptuously between them. He preaches with wild gestures, like the philosophy of industrialism come to life. His slick hair shines of oil. His suit fills me with a sense of superiority—our autos, our pocket radios, our cheap plastic toys, our sneaky-petes, our hairdressers.
    It reminds me of that postcard. Grandma Wallpaper sent me a postcard of her new eighteen-inch purple mohawk and her new tattoo. The new tattoo on her neck is a three-quarter view of a bulldozer with the word "Trouble" clearly spelled out underneath it in a fine palatino type. It matches

i'm right here

the tattoo on the other side of her neck—a Big Mac with the inscription "Nature Against Man" below it.

She sent it in a four-foot by eight-foot envelope, so I wouldn't miss it in the mail. I have a tendency to ignore my mail for as long as humanly possible. The large envelope was fashioned from the delicate wings of a hundred butterflies to give it that special translucent/kaleidoscope/stained-glass feel. As a respectful nod to the past, she had riveted it together with bolts from the Hindenburg.

The postcard was accidentally delivered to someone I vaguely know, someone I slightly resemble, and just as he was taking the postcard from the mailwoman's fingers, he got creamed by a car by mistake. As he lay on the blacktop, his dying words wobbling as they surfed that last weak breath, he yet again ridiculed my imagination. And again offered no viable alternative. A passerby snatched the postcard from his fading clutches as he died into it. The postcard eventually ended up playing a prominent role in a motor oil advertisement, spiritually enhancing our already comically rich lives.

I have long been suspicious of the postal service. Not the institution itself, mind you, but the general concept of mail. I'm always afraid someone will eventually take an envelope I happen to send and use my saliva from the seal to clone me. Hey, I've seen it happen.

The bowling alley depresses me. No action. I drop a dime. I go visit Justin. The front door of his white two-story Leave-It-to-Beaver is cinder-blocked, so I have to enter through the sterile, two-hundred-foot-long concrete "Dr. Strangelove" tunnel which runs from a drainage ditch under the neighborhood to his boiler room down in his paranoidally deep basement which drops a staggering eighty feet below the surface.

At the end of the starkly lit tunnel is not a door, but a shower curtain, mold and all. There is no bell to ring. No knocker to knock. You must yodel, and yodel your heart out, in order to be heard and gain admittance. The yodeling is carried through the two-story by way of the peaceful sheet metal heating ducts. Of course the chanting also drifts down the tunnel to hum and warble out of the various sewers and drains in the area, prompting local legends of haunting ghosts and sneaky little green people.

There's a hint of a song in the air, buzzing in the distance. I concentrate. I know this one. Why, it's Black Flag's "What I See." It makes me feel welcome. It makes me feel at home. I bob my head to the friendly greeting. "Who are you to tell me that I'm wrong?... I close my eyes..." The tune gently melts into James Brown's "Sex Machine." I bob my head. "... Get on up ... Get on up ..."

Justin answers my yodel by parting the disgusting shower curtain. He stands before me wearing only a simple silvery suit of armor. Alas, it breaks my heart, an old Romanian one from the barbarians of the 14th century. It has recently been restored, complete with a small plastic air-conditioning unit mounted on the back of the helmet. It hums comfortingly.

"Hit me," he greets. "Go ahead, you know you want to." His words are faint and muffled. "Take off your belt, go ahead," he prods, tapping my shoulder clumsily with his metal fingers. "Come on."

Being the guest, I feel polite etiquette would dictate me to indulge my good host. I pull off my world championship belt, bring it from behind my back, and whip it over my head to wallop him on the shoulder. The thick leather slaps the armor with an echoing "bonk" sound—after all, It's my good world championship belt, not the cheap vinyl one.

i'm right here

Muffled laughter escapes the ornate iron mask which is perforated with fabulous mythically dark holes. I recoil and swing back around, this time arching my back and throwing my legs and shoulders and all my weight into it. But the blow just ricochets off the armor again, the momentum causing the diminutive Justin to backpedal several steps. "Not bad," he muffles. "Hey, try on my little green suit. You can leap about in it—in and out of the shadows and mist. The old people and the impressionable are out in force tonight. Let's go start some rumors." He reaches around with a soft clank-clank and stiffly raises one of his aluminum jet packs. He takes a few steps forward, closes the curtain and turns to start back down the tunnel. "Now let's hit that bowling alley and get us some pooder."

I can't help thinking to myself, enviously, as we walk, "Man, Justin, you sure do got style."

I always have the option of killing you

"I just got off work," he says as he unbuttons his overcoat before me. He turns and steps to the living room, looking to the open window across the room and continuing to unbutton. "I just got back," he tells me as he is looking down at his hands. He stands at the edge of the linoleum, balancing on the brink of the living room and the cusp of the kitchen, straddling the opposing forces of the two, bringing them together in a collision of logic and good taste.

He grew up on an apple orchard, but now lives in this small apartment and drives a city bus. He married an heir to a zipper magnate, then left her for an heir to a paper clip fortune. But that was a long time ago. Neither of the relationships lasted, always too much emphasis on bringing little things together, holding them in place. He has had major problems with paper clips ever since—and you won't find a zipper anywhere near him. I guess he just didn't want to dwell on things like that, so he decided to pull things apart. Through the years, life had had a way of filing him down until he was just an average Joe. He was a museum piece, the real thing. Uncle Hate was a lumberjack who had lost all confidence in his ability. He stung a guy with one of those long

i'm right here

chain saws a few years back. That's when he moved back and was more or less swallowed by the city.

He turns and opens his coat to reveal a T-shirt and a ring of thick, red sticks strapped around his chest like a cummerbund. But it is not a cummerbund; it is a strand of dynamite taped to his belly, bandaged around his midsection as if holding him together.

I look at his midsection as he reaches to hang his coat on a hook on the kitchen wall. He looks across the formica table at me and then down to his stomach. "Oh, this," he says. "Just dynamite," he explains, as if it couldn't hurt anyone. Then he turns and walks calmly into the living room.

I hear him in the other room. He is shuffling around, moving a box or dragging a bag across the floor. "I carry a bagful at work, on the bus and stuff. This is just my extra, just in case." His voice is muffled against the back side of the wall that divides the rooms. I can't see him so I have to step out of the kitchen, across the old peach linoleum with little baby blue kidney shapes floating in it.

I peek around the wall that divides the horrifyingly stereotypical kitchen and am immersed in the deathly boring living room. It is so horrible I can't even scream, so sad, so typical, so banal as to crush me. I feel different, disconnected, as if my head is stuck on someone else's body.

"I keep most of it in a brown paper bag," he continues. "Along with a copy of the *Catcher in the Rye* and some pro Castro leaflets." He is down on one knee, reaching into a wrinkled shopping bag next to the fireplace. He pulls his hand out of the bag and pitches a copy of the *Catcher in the Rye* into the deep, open mouth of the fireplace. He reaches in the bag and quickly pulls out another and tosses it in. Some jazzy music jumps out of the old plastic radio on the windowsill and skips wildly about the room—Sonny Rollins, I think.

I always have the option

He shoves his hand in the bag again and flips in another and another. Some of them are newer than others, but they're all in pretty bad shape, all tattered and worn, all faded, some healing with yellowing scotch tape.

"Man," he says, shaking his head. "Sometimes..." He gazes into the blank emptiness. "Sometimes I'd like to snuff some of them out, those walking dead.... And any fool who pulls a knife on me—I'll let 'em know I got no problem with taking us both out—I'll tell him to bring it on, 'cause I've been looking forward to it." He speaks to himself as the music spins around frantically, lots of little noises, a supermarket of tiny noises, running around hysterically, like children who don't have control of their devilish little bodies.

    Dump Dump   bliddily-deep   Bap, Bap, Bap, Bap   Blaaaa Na-na
Dumb-dumb-dumb   **bliddily**-deep   Blaaaahhh Nah-nah
    Dumb-dumb-dumb   bliddily-deep   Bla Nah   Blaaaahhh Na-na
Dump Dump   boom boom boom   **Wah Nah Nah**   Doop-Doop-Doop-Doop
        Dumb-dumb-dumb   bliddily-deep   Blaaaa Na-na
Dumb-dumb-dumb   **Wah Na Na**   Whhhhaaaaaa   Bap, Bap, Bap, Bap

And I have to just sit in it and take it—that sissy-britches wise-ass music forcing itself into me.

He stands and brushes off his knees. "I've got to wire some more of them suckers off," he says, but I lose him in the music. It seemed to say: "Do you want to work in a factory, do you want to work in a factory with me? Oooh yeah. Lose a finger. Lose a finger. Lose a finger with meeeeee. Oooooh yeah. Bloody-stump. Bloody-stump. Boom boom boom boom. Take this guy's wallet. Take this guy's wallet. Slit his throat with some piano wire—yeaaaah. Boom boom boom boom..."

Stan Kenton, I think.

I stand in the middle of the room, enjoying the suggestive, subversive nature of the composition. I enjoy the fact that it can turn me on to crime, that *it* can enjoy the fact that

i'm right here

it can turn me on to crime. Or that it can just as simply kill my spirit through the waste of repetitious, arbitrary labor.

I step backward, working my way over to the plastic radio growing on the sill in the corner. I brush against it, sitting myself on the sill to force it out the window. A silent moment later, its plastic smacks against the brick wall, about five feet down, as the cord tightened. I lean down and slide my hand down my leg, down the painter's pants I'm wearing, to reach the cord, and with one good tug, I jerk that sucker from the wall socket. I feel the weight of that radio hang in the cold air; it reminds me of all the suggestions it has whispered. I let it sink closer to the sidewalk. I hear it scrape against the rough brick, getting heavier and heavier as I sit back up. *What the hell*, I think, and I let go.

The cord zips through my hand, runs straight up my arm, and leaps out the window, out into the cold air. There is a brief, enjoyable pause before I hear the radio *clack* hollowly against the metal roof of a car below.

I cross my legs and watch him lumber into the kitchen as if I were watching his entire life. *So your wife left town with my wife...* —as if I were still watching it happen, playing it out in slow motion before my eyes, every detail pulsating slowly, over and over, as if I can reach out and grab it.

I watch the guy, that lump of a man, Uncle Hate, a tumor of a man, a one-celled amoeba of a man, a dripping faucet of a man—with his pictures on the fridge, of Aunt Cookie and Cousin Splatter, and Ammonia and Mingus and Yeah, still in jail sniffing CO_2, I suppose, with my twin sisters, Catheter and Meat, and my mother, Alopecia, who liked her men small, preferably fast-talking salesmen, picnicking with the neighbor, Climidia, and her twins, Laramie and Laredo, and their live-in lovers, Kuala Lumpur and Ketosis, planning the prison break, wringing their hands over the instability of science and the absurdity of reason.

I sigh and swallow and look around. I am so bored. I feel like I've been waiting in the apartment my entire life, like I'm stuck in that quicksand air. I'm restless, fidgeting, rubbing my legs and arms, crossing my legs again, crossing my arms, running my hands through my dry hair, but everything is still moving in slow motion.

I'm tied up, stuck in someone else's body, stuck in your world—and just wait till I get my paws on you. I sigh again and exhale and think of how limiting my options are. I have no history or tradition to draw on for direction. I'm a cultural bastard—with no vowels in my name, no neighborhood, no hometown, nothing to cling to, not anything.

I lean out the window, catching some of that cold biting air. I look over my shoulder, out at all the jagged rooftops, angled reds and greens, blacks and browns. I remember fights I've gotten into, out there in that tight two-story city—from when I was little to when I was sticking that first guy in a bar and kicking him in the head over and over, just because no one would stop me, as if it were all for them. They just stood around. I don't know, maybe they were afraid of me or something. I remember that guy's face. I'll always remember that drowsy, soupy look in his eyes when I was kicking him.

Some people I didn't know joined in. What the hell. We dragged him into the bathroom. I kicked him while this hairy guy muzzled his face by leaning down on one of those big rubber plungers. Another hairy guy worked on him with one of his own shoes. That hairy guy was one of those intellectual pit bulls. They called him "The Preacher." He was spouting logarithms for further humiliation, shouting

i'm right here

deep into the soupy guy's soupy face, browbeating him into submission: "Explain e=mc^2! . . . What is the annual rainfall of Clovis, Idaho?" We shared him. And had a groin-kickin' good time, one and all.

And then going to that job interview at that plastic factory a few years later and having him turn out to be the boss. He knew right away. I know he did. Looking back I could see it in his eyes. I knew something was up. I knew it, like I knew him from somewhere, but just couldn't pin down where. From when I was younger, church maybe, the Marines maybe. The Marines made men of us, maybe. Together, I thought. Then he stepped out of his small musty office for a second and walked back in with some big guys and they kicked the crap outta me. I remember that. They bounced me off the old walls. I remember that well; you just don't forget a thing like that.

They drove me out of town and dumped my limp body into a swampy ditch. "*This* is the 'Preacher Man,'" he explained, as one of his bigger, hairier goons spouted scripture and worked on me with a spatula.

After they tired, they meditated over my limp body. Then they got up and left. Just up and left me out there. Damn, I admired that.

There's a clock ticking loudly on the shelf. A cheap plastic one, chirping away like my life. I reach over and pick it up. I hold it. I roll it over and over in my hands. I close my eyes. The clock feels clean and cheap, with clear-baby-blue-sky American optimism. I flip it over my shoulder, the cord snapping out of the plug and jumping through the air enthusiastically.

I lean against the window jamb and cross my legs again, looking down at my work boots, waiting for that

I always have the option

smiling second, that artistic heartbreaking pause of anticipation, my heart stopping until that faint *clack* of plastic careening off concrete calls up to me.

I pull some drill bits out of my pocket. They are thin and smooth, entangled in lint. I brought them home from work today—why the hell not. I run my finger down them, bounce them in my palm. I flip them over my shoulder. They take a long time, but some things take a long time, sometimes you have to be patient and wait for things to develop. Finally, they let me know how they are doing. Finally, I hear them tinkling up to me against the wishes of metal and cement, those egotistical phonies.

I sigh and stand and reach out to the simple pine shelf floating on cheap, thin, metal brackets that remind me of my uncle. He's in the small, brutally ugly kitchen now. How he can stand that excruciating torment I don't know, with its hollow screaming poisonous innocence and insane linoleum walls and cabinets and ceiling, making me all the more impatient, like I've been waiting here forever.

I hitch up my pants, then grip the wood shelf with both hands and hold it, feeling its smoothness, catching the fresh, tangy, biting smell of its flesh as it rushes through my body. I lift it up and it tilts in my arms for a moment as I steady it. I sample its heft. I feel its honesty. I lift it to my eyes and drop it slowly back down to my waist, its trinkets wobble nervously, trustingly—the enema bags, the breast pump, a bottle of eradicator, a rambling 300-page love letter written in German and typed in thin, stark letters, all of Satan's junk mail, his lumberjack photos, and, finally, his finger bobbing in the golden liquid of a baby food jar.

I swing around and walk it over to the window, holding it for a moment in the breeze. I look back into the kitchen and then set it free. I let it drop into the air and watch it float gently down into the day, quivering down to the car below.

"What was *that?*" My uncle peeked his big head from the kitschy kitchen. "I don't know," I say, paging through the yellowing science fiction paperback in my lap. I sit on the sill, the fog of stench reaching to me from the kitchen. Its aroma wraps around me, drawing the walls in to smother me with its thick, abrasive air; a stew of smells—bleach, old oil, rusting metal sky, standing against me, waiting to attack.

Man, I really gotta get myself outta here. I picture myself leaning back, leaning back farther, into the thin day, into its last icy breath of thin air. It sucks me in, my head swimming dizzy twists of sky, forcing me down like when I was younger, when I was a kid and would swing on the swings, holding my head back in disorientation, my stomach gulping, my brain gasping as the school yard twisted and shredded with the sky in blurring, rushing strands of burning color.

I stand and turn to take in some fresh air. Pots and pans clank, a spoon scrapes a plate, and I toss the book out into the air, an offering to fate, as if it belonged out there. The pulpy paperback spins softly down to the street. I look out at the sky, feeling as though it is my home, the only place that I can trust, that I have any ties to, the only place I can call my own. And finally I spot my dirigible approaching out of the stirring, gray emptiness. My smile could not be contained by the room, by the apartment, or by the city at the sight of my tremendous airship—humming closer, reverberating through the air, fluttering in my chest, and shaking the neighborhood. I wave, signaling it, as it nears. The long silver zeppelin floats above the rooftops with tender, angular shadows creep-

I always have the option

ing, slowly turning into position. Its slender shadow slithers up the building to finally cover me.

"Hey, where'd the shelf go!" I hear Uncle Hate exclaim as I reach up to the window jamb. I step up on the sill. I pull myself up and step out into the day, grabbing the thick oily rope my crew had dangled down to me.

I drift off the ledge and hang in the air for a moment, spinning slowly in the grayness, watching my uncle getting bigger and bigger as he rushes across the floor to the window, a pot jiggling in one outstretched hand, an enema bag held high in the other, the apron of dynamite still secured by the electrician's tape, hugging him with a silvery metal smile.

Later, as we climb over the ocean, we sail above an albino Gotha bomber out on patrol, probably out looking for us. Its escort, an Albatross two winger, sputters out of the fog to challenge us. My crew returns fire as the beautiful machine approaches, its round fuselage candy-striped with painted sugar-stick swirls of yellows and reds that spin around its delicate fabric. I am bedazzled. I clutch my chest and almost cry, watching in amazement as it makes two or three passes, lazily looping around my airship before finally breaking off to sputter away hypnotically in the droning hum of a giant bumblebee. My crew pleads to launch countermeasures. They say they've got the S.E.5a ready to go, but I am too overcome by its wonder to have it destroyed.

That evening I sit on the sill in one of the finely crafted aluminum windows that line the metal cabin slung under the long frame of the ship. I feel the ship holding me up. I feel the distance of air beneath us. It seems like miles, like I hold those miles in my hand. I feel it in my conscious, bobbing me ever so slightly, as if floating on an innertube in some calm, dark water. I close my eyes to feel that calm distance, as if I were that distance—as if I always had been that distance, that heavy, wet air.

"I always have the option of killing you," I shrug, filing a thin shank of metal with an old family photo album of yours. "My government has graciously bestowed upon me that option if the need presents itself," I instruct, and gaze out at the long fraying fingers of cloud rushing by. You stretch your legs, trying to adjust your seat. I've got you tied to the dreamy gold wood and promising gray metal of an old school chair. You're secured tightly, warmly, with silvery thick electrician's tape. I'm flaunting that sweater of yours, I'm wearing it proudly, that red and yellow candy-striped 1960s ski sweater you wore in that old Roman gladiator film, *The Viking Queen*, I believe.

"It's looking like a nice, long trip," I say. I turn and reach my head out the window, the cold air stinging my cheeks. I survey the sky above, clutching the silver metal jamb as I lean out, reading a path in the clouds. I lean back in against the side of the window lazily and reach out to let the fuzzy strings of white cloud whistle through my hand. I toss the photo album out the window. It spins slowly as it disappears into the mist. "We're going to try to deprogram you—they happen to think you're worth converting . . ." I sigh. "Personally, I feel they're mistaken."

and

Dad was an alcoholic. Which is to say he was powerless over the liquid. "Blood" he called it. He was its servant; it was his master. It was really hard on the family, as you can imagine. After years of ugly messes—many quite public—we finally licked the problem. But we had to do it together. What finally did it was that we made him wear a half pint of agonizingly smooth twelve-year-old scotch around his neck all day. It was secured by a heavy steel chain that we got at my cousin's hardware store. Dad picked out the one he liked best. Upon the silver chain we had engraved all the prayers to a complete rosary. I was informed later that this gesture was a great comfort. I can imagine it was. It's always the little touches, isn't it. Well, that, and it helped that the bottle was attached to a series of wires that looped around his waist and into a corresponding paddle-locked knapsack that was stuffed full of dynamite.

I tap my pen. Tap tap tappa ta tap tap. I always tap my pen. Tappa-ta tap tap tappa-tappa. I'm always tapping that pen. Tappa tap tappa tap tap. My fluent, jazzy music blooms from my lyrical wand. All day long. I've always been quite proficient and I've become very good. It's one of those

i'm right here

things that came easy to me. Enthusiastic, I recorded an album, but for some reason it failed miserably and I had to move back into that old musty silo that tilts in the middle of that overgrown alfalfa field at the edge of town, where cleaning consisted of bagging up the beer bottles and throwing the occasional bucket of soapy water into the outhouse, where I would sit on the ratty old couch, stroking my sexy goiter and smoking pot and watching television all day long—what we in the business call "waiting for our big break."

The radio sadistically overplays a really bad song. It makes me want to start little fires. That radio station is in imminent danger. I grip the wheel tighter, clench my teeth, turn into the oncoming traffic, swerve to avoid a city bus, and head for the gas station across the street. I'm up on two wheels, careening, with one hand on the wheel, a cigarette dangling from my lips.

You died last night. It's morning now. The sun is bright. My glasses are lying on your dresser, but you're not anywhere, because you're gone, you're nowhere, real gonesville, man, real squaresville, real L-7, man. You're dead and I slept in your bed last night with a swinging flight attendant in from Akron.

All my life I dreamed of being an architect, of designing great cathedrals. I'd lie in the grass on my back on summer days and watch the clouds drift by, watching the cathedrals slowly grow and change.
    I'd build great rooms and wonderful spaces with fantastic views. I'd close my eyes and feel great libraries rise up out of my palms, great museums leap from my quivering hands, monuments jump from my shaking arms. I wanted to

and

go to school and become that architect. I'd be motivated. And I'd be well-rounded in design and materials and construction. But as things developed, I got a job with a contractor. And that was just fine—I could still sit and tend to those monuments, those museums to humanity, I could still sit and watch them grow. But due to the flat economy the only work I could get was the building and renovating of gay bathhouses, massage parlors, and brothels—homes for the quiet, the lonely, the desperate, the moping. I enjoyed the work and made a treasure of new friends.

At my last job interview, the fellow comfortably seated across the desk from me asked, "How far would you go for this company?" Something like that, anyway. So I thought for a moment and settled back in my chair and said something like: "I'll do whatever it takes." Or wait, no. That's not it. I know. I remember now. What I did was I sat and brooded for a moment, then set my hand up on his desk and brought my other hand slamming down upon it, impaling myself on his desk with his letter opener.
 I stared at that letter opener, peeking out of the top of my hand for a few seconds, then I leaned forward and whispered, "That's how far I'll go, Jasper."
 A tetanus shot later, and I started that afternoon.

My girlfriend is afraid that she's starting to lose it. What she fears is losing herself. In the future, this will become a very common concern. She was there once, and then she got busy, and then she was gone. She started slipping away. Too many hours at work, too many hours with me. And then she had lost herself.
 To try to get herself back she's been hanging pictures of herself up all over her apartment. Now there are dozens of

i'm right here

her all around, and more appearing everyday. When she leaves, she carries a hand mirror with her, to always check to see if she's still there—on the bus, at work, in the movie theater, in bed with me.

". . . mapping uncharted regions of the psyche and society's elevation of the rational over the incomprehensible. Truck stops are art! Make love in them!" I wander around town, insisting with taut gestures. It's a thing I do. ". . . Strip malls are physical manifestations of shame and guilt. They're a cry for help—a plea from the city planners who are commissioned to protect us from such vulgarities . . . We are, as they say, as far from the truth as we ever were . . . An angry man is someone who hasn't given up yet . . . You know you're old when you no longer get bummed out about things . . . I didn't have a date for the prom and now I'm really pissed . . ." I stare ahead, at some unseen object, at some elusive, past event. ". . . I feel the presence of time on the street. Time, that sneaky bastard . . . Words are missing. Words flee my mouth like the squealing little pigs they are. Words stab me in the back like the cowards they are. Realism never got any of us anywhere. It never attended the funeral of a friend. It never asked that cute girl from the bus stop out on a date. It never took a vicious beating for anyone. It never took a bullet for the president . . . She sterilizes me with her perceptions—towing my psychological car—repossessing my mental Winnebago—hauling bits of my psyche away and dumping them in some lonely, moldy ditch on the edge of town . . . I can't seem to accept the way things are . . . I can't seem to come to terms with this place . . ." I wander the streets, blinking spastically, my mouth a rubber band, my mind the carburetor of an old ice cream truck, my eyes two grandmothers arguing on a city bus. ". . . My first child is going to be conceived on Frank

and

Gehry's lawn ... Grass makes me cry. Sky makes me want to smell the socks of strangers down at the bus station. The city's sublime burbling babble makes me feel like an unwilling participant in such an accelerated world . . ." I had been as content as I had ever been, as happy as I could ever think to be. I had lived in a tent in the bright green woods. Alone at the edge of a clear, bubbling creek. In company with the epic, rippling water. But then I got my ass busted—for having opinions, for conjuring ideas, for inciting thought, for "insisting with taut gestures", a heinous offense.

I recall that it was about to rain. The sky was pretty, in its delicate heaviness—murky gray-blue quiet, and the townies worked me over good before the cops and inmates got their turn. And then I spent my days in the company of the galactic, hollow echo of a small dripping sink.

It was at the trial that I was charged with two counts of "Loud boringness" and one count "Conspicuous mediocrity in the second degree." Paradoxically, after the sentencing— of 1000 hours of *Gilligan's Island* and *I Dream of Jeannie* reruns (Gilligan being the Christ figure; and Jeannie, the outcast, a slave to the social expectations of the day)—the jury members each patted me on the back saying, "Keep up the good work," and sent me on my way.

The love of my life ran off with a midget. It hurt me deeply and really bummed me out. He was a stripper, after all. But they prefer to be referred to as "exotic dancers," don't they.

I was hanging out with the adults, as I'm known to do on occasion, and ... I don't know why I do these things, but for some reason I just picked up my boss and began twirling him above my head like a baton.

49

i'm right here

I whirled him around and around in a windmill fashion, and, for some reason, in wide-eyed wonder, I shouted, "Look at the little guy go!!"

I considered spinning him by an arm and a leg, administering an "airplane ride," but then that little man in my head who tells me to watch pro wrestling and use the terms "booty" and "boogie" a lot, advised me to grab him by his little ankles and spin him. I heeded the advice, and, to my pleasant surprise, several adjectives flowed, quickly spurting from my glee-encrusted face, flicking across the boardroom: "Squirt! Runt! Pipsqueak!" as if my height were some sort of reward that I had earned, my smile a medal I deserved, my clothes a tribute, my sports car an honorarium, my blond hair a trophy, my blue eyes an award that I had worked hard to achieve.

The secretaries rose from their chairs in the back. "Put George down," they pleaded. "Put George down," they demanded. "He's, he's, he's getting dizzy," they pointed. "Look at his face, it's all red." The other ass-kissers scrambled behind the phallic boardroom table, scurrying in the phallic office tower. "Stop twirling George." At that I bent him over my knee and announced, "I'm a gonna spank the daylights outta the li'l devil!"

Some of the associates tried to pry him away. I pulled back. "Come 'ere ya gnome-like little troll." Then I took off his tiny shoes and stuffed them down my pants.

Several minutes later, as the security guards dragged me out, I made some rather unique comments to the boss, such as: "So long, Peewee!" and "I bet when you hear piccolo music you do an uncontrollable little jig" and "I bet you've got a pair of those little green shoes for your cute little feet—the ones with the jangly bells and toes that curl up on the ends" and "I bet you live under a little bridge in the forest." and, as I gripped the doorjamb while the security personnel tugged on me, I stuck my head back into the room and said, "You write like a girl."

Someone pulled out a frying pan and took a step toward me. I ran out like a sniveling coward and jumped into the waiting warm arms of the hulking security men.

Then, as they dragged me past the receptionist's desk and out the glass doors to the elevators, for some reason I began bleating like a lamb: "Baaaa baaaahhh. Baaaaaaa baaaaa," and then I wiggled one arm free and loosened my belt and dropped my pants.

As the elevator doors closed, I stuck my head out and shouted, "Oh yeah, one more thing, some of you guys can really stink up the ol' bathroom, if ya know what I mean!"

I don't know why I do those kinds of things sometimes. I guess because it was my last day there anyway, so I figured what the hell—I'd give them all a little thrill, something to talk about, something to remember me by.

It's sad to watch someone without something they once had—trying to hold on, trying to get it back. People lose themselves, you know. My girlfriend is losing herself—slowly slipping away—what she once was, what she always thought herself to be, what she always aspired to, what she had hoped to become.

I know her, you see, so I can see through her sadness. I can see through it enough to think myself lucky. I think, "Wow, how darling. How splendid. How unique in all the world. What a gal," as she puts up mirrors all over her apartment so as not to lose herself. As to remind her of who she is, of who she was, of who she could be. To remind her that

i'm right here

she is here—that she is very much here, all around, more and more appearing everyday.

I ran into a "writer" friend of mine—tony rauchaRauchaRaucha. He was selling some of his stories on the sidewalk. He had set up a flimsy old card table. It was bandaged together with duct tape. In the middle of the table was a sign that mumbled in crayon: "stories $1". The sign leaned against a thick candle that pinned a stack of stories down against the wind.

I knew an old girlfriend of his who had bought the candle for him at a garage sale many years ago. Some couple was divorcing and thus had to have the sale as they were leaving their house. Their wedding vows encircled the candle.

"I'm a painter," he said, introducing himself as if he'd never seen me before. "And these are some of my paintings, only written down." He was wearing a ripped T-shirt that was freckled with yawning moth holes and acned with tiny paint splatters.

"Oh," I said.

"I have four three-pagers today. They took me years to complete. I have fossilized my fears, put them down—fears, fears, fears. Fears and dreams. Put them down so they'll stay put for a while, for safekeeping—statues of dreams and ideas that'll outlive us all."

"Oh, sure." I nodded.

"Let's see, today I've got *You're My Problem, Asswipe*, *Will You Beat the Crap Outta Me, Please*, and *I Was Intimidated by Her Breasts*. The composition *His Testicles Exploded* is on special . . . which is to say it's free," he shrugged. "The authorities in town thought it best for everyone involved if I decided to get a hobby, so here I am," he nodded.

and

"Yes, yes, authorities can be like that—"

"Indeed," he interrupted, watching an old milk truck roll by. He stood up from his peach crate and saluted the truck as it passed. "I also have the two 300-page chapbooks I wrote that study these four stories in depth: *Swinging from the Meat Hook* and *The Death of Literature*. I also have a poorly mimeographed copy of my first book, *Release the Monkeys: an Elvis Adventure*— an erotic homage to the King, if you will," he shrugged. "Like I said, the cops told me I needed something to do—and I like writing, writing being the sincerest form of exaggeration," he looked up at the sky and tilted his head. "Lately I've been composing more introspective, exploratory pieces, mostly for railroad publications— you know, periodicals, regional journals, historical societies, and the like. Basically, I can say anything I want, as long as I mention railroads every once in a while.

"I used to write more jazzy, experimental stuff— documenting the episodic incongruities of life—but all that hyper-fiction was just making me hyper, so I started in on more *imaginative* fiction—one of the more disreputable forms of writing, just below the court summons, traffic ticket, or ransom note . . ."

I nodded, trying to step away.

". . . but, to be honest, I guess I just long to write a really nice sentence." He looked up at the sky again. "Writing, as they say, is like tending a garden; you have to weed it and weed it, it takes a long time to grow a good story . . . but then again, there's some pretty swingin' shit in there," he tapped his hand on a stack of papers.

"Why do you do this?" I asked him in a slight whisper, but the question seemed more like one of those that I was really trying to ask of myself.

i'm right here

"Oh, lots of reasons, I suppose—nothing better to do, I guess. Also, I just can't stand all that slick crap that's put out there now. All those tragedy stories. All that depressing drivel. All those stories of people taking advantage of other people, of weak people exploiting weaker people. Somehow I don't view being a victim as being admirable or heroic.

"It all just ends up being *People* magazine literature—nothing is left to interpretation or to the imagination. And there seems little room in any of those pieces for reflection or contemplation. They're not about ideas, really, they're about intrusion . . . voyeurism . . . gossip. It's nothing more than . . . than . . . than emotional pornography, as far as I'm concerned."

"You wrote those books, huh?" I asked, against my better judgement.

"Yes, and I am deeply ashamed of myself—there's some filthy, filthy language in there," he tapped one of the piles with his finger.

"OK," I said stepping back.

"I've been a very naughty boy . . . I think I need a spanking."

I took a few more steps back.

"Will you spank me?"

"Ah, no."

"Can I sleep in your basement tonight?" he said with his hands cupped around his mouth.

"Well, I gotta fly."

"Here . . ." He stuck out the Elvis book. "I just can't seem to get rid of any of them today . . ."

"I'll lend a hand!" I turned and stepped up, lifting the table. The candle rolled off and dropped down into a mud puddle. Some mud splashed up on his painter's pants and the papers scattered to blow down the street.

and

He stared down the block, watching the papers blow away. "Thanks." He shrugged as I set the rickety table back down. He had a confused, disappointed look on his face, but you know how moody those crazy artists get.

I thought for a moment as I witnessed the papers drifting out of sight. "I don't know why I do these things," I finally sighed.

The writer watched for a moment, too, then said, "Good."

I just stood there and thought about candles and tables and fears—and I thought about *that* candle, and about *that* table, and about *his* fears. But mostly all I could think of was how much I longed, just for once, to have a regular life. There's got to be a better life out there for me, there's just got to be.

And somehow, somewhere, there's just got to be a good person buried deep down inside of me. Somewhere, somehow, there's just got to be a place for me. There's just got to be a nice person hidden deep within me.

That night I was spirited away on the wings of a gastric journey. Tempt me with their seductive "all you can eat," will they. Silly fools.

I licked my fingers as I crawled through the ventilation duct, sneaking out on yet another of life's little bills. And when I got home, I could hear the old lady down the hall—the gentle hum of her accordion calling out to me. And there I was, you know, murderin' germs in my bathroom again, like the germ-jukin' junky that I am. But that warbling hum had its grip on me. I sighed and looked down, lamenting the fact that, in the end, there's only so much you can do. You can only get a toilet so clean; in the end it is still just a toilet.

The humming subsided, that hollow hum, so I cracked

i'm right here

my door, crouched down, and caught the old tattooed lady ducking out again. She was wearing one of her impressive trench coats, with stolen paint cans rattling magically in the deep pockets. Her graffiti would bring tears to your eyes.

I would greatly appreciate if she would stop playing her accordion so late at night, making up songs about sex, death, and murder. And I prefer she not write all those songs about me, about my vapid existence, predicting my demise—my downfall. It's a personal thing, I suppose—it's *my* demise, after all.

The ice in the glass plays tricks of perception and scale. The cubes are mumbling, spreading the truth: life is a psychological clambake—ignore it as best you can.

As for me, well, I'm just sitting here at the end of the bar again. It's about 10:45. Plenty of time to do whatever I can, if I could only figure out what that could be. I'm looking into the glass. It's dark all around. The glass seems to repel the darkness. I feel the ice—that the ice is me, and I'm just sitting here in the slow quiet, all stoked up for some really "underwear-hanging-from-the-lamp-shade,-don't-even-know-where-my-pants-are" type sex. But here I sit, alone, trapped in this glass again.

Pretty soon my girlfriend's floors and ceilings are all mirrors. I was scared pissless. Then, I stopped over one time and, thank God, most of the mirrors were down. "I'm so happy for you," I gushed in relief. Standing in the doorway, I beamed at her as she knitted in her chair in the living room. "Thank goodness you've found who you are again!" I held my face in excitement.

"That oughtta do it." She snapped her gum as her knitting needles clickitty-clacked. She motioned her head to the window beside her.

I bent down slightly to peer out, and sure enough, there she was out there, big as life. She had rented the tremendous billboard atop the building across the street. She'd put her smiling face on it—all one hundred feet of it. And it stares in on her and her little life, it stares in through her tiny windows, looking in on her, checking up on herself as she knits, watching as she reads, as she cooks, as she does her dishes, as she sleeps at night.

We got into a fight. She's thinking of leaving town. She says she needs to find herself. I said, "Haven't we been through all this with the mirror thing and all?" But she said, "That was different! I have dreams, you know."

I know calling her was probably a bad idea, but if I did the right thing all the time . . . well, I just wouldn't have any fun now, would I? I don't mind trouble, it makes me feel alive. She wasn't home so I left a message on her machine—a simple threat, the kind she always enjoyed: "If you don't call me back, I'll show up at your work and run around naked, shouting your name."

I had nothing more to do, so I decided to take a walk down by the river. The park was concealed by snow. Wrapped in that envelope. Effeminately superimposed in that sloppy way. Smeared in that greasy, scaly veneer. Paved with it's brittle paper. A really disgraceful job if you ask me.

Whisks of radiant white kissed the abyss of dispirited sky like a screened-in porch. The deep luminous blue yawned above, reaching to search beyond all my possibilities. The snow was a dull white, a hapless victim. The trees glowed the shiny silver of ice in the setting sun. It was all so quiet and still and calm. The natural beauty began to take over. I became imbued with truth. I thought about her and wished she were here. I could feel her all around. I could feel her

i'm right here

inside of me. I could feel her rummaging around, rearranging my mental furniture, rattling my pipes, trying on my clothes, making long-distance phone calls without permission . . .

But somehow I just knew there was nothing I could say to pull her back, nothing I could do to keep her here. Her deep, flinty voice still echoing in my dreams . . . her delicate ears still warming my cheeks . . . her arms like rivers, her eyes like clouds, her whisper sleeping in my heart . . . I couldn't lose her. Such a part of me. I'd be lost without her.

I started dropping off my jacket as I carefully breathed her purity and stillness, as if my skin were trying to crawl off of me and get away. "I'm right here, God, can't you see me? I'm right here!" I shouted for help. "Why won't you help me? I'm right here."

Pieces of me peeled and slid off. Hypnotically, I began to shed. Almost immediately people began to collect, politely trying to cover me in that concerned, Midwestern manner. I twisted and broke free and galloped—pushing them aside, stiff-arming, knocking some of them down. I ran to her. I ran and ran. They found me naked in her closet, curled up on the floor, shivering.

The way I figure it, if they can take a girl like that away, well then what's the point?

little fires

I'll probably end up writing for tv someday

Chill ribbon boy, slinger. Bop sway bop in your big jeans up to here. I'll make sure it's nice and tight. Seriously flawed—low, like up for two days low. On the toad low. Pissing in my butt job low. Line them shiny ones up Shawanda. Crazy, maybe.

See, I could do that.

roy's the devil

Today while getting a radiator flush we found out that our friend Roy is actually Satan.

"Roy's the devil," Becky suddenly blurted out.

The rest of us sat stunned.

I stopped flipping through the hunting magazine on my lap. Tommy let the car magazine slide off his lap and crumple against the floor. Becky's prophetic words echoed in the small, bright cinder-block waiting room. Her words seemed to seep gradually into the walls, crawling away from the rest of us as if to hide like tiny animals.

In the center of each wall in that painfully square room hung an 8"x10" black-and-white autopsy photo of President Kennedy. Each picture rested in its own thin black frame.

"Yes, ah-ha," we all nodded in surprised agreement. "That does make a lot of sense. Roy is . . . Roy is the devil."

My gold 1974 Ford Pinto hung above us on the hydraulic lift. A sanctified idol. A sacrifice. An offering. It hung like a metal coffin. It hung at the mercy of the mechanics. They seemed apathetic to our fate. Just one more old car, I

roy's the devil

guess. Just one more greasy number on a clipboard. Just one more clutch Roy had burned out.

"Yes," I finally agreed, staring through the dirty little window, siding with everyone else for a change. My eyes narrowed. "Roy is the Antichrist."

"I thought that was Henry Ford," popped Smedly as he looked up from his textbook.

"Shut the fuck up, you pimply heap of goat droppings," I advised. "You're always thinking too much."

"I thought it was Henry Ford and his chariot to abomination, the automobile," he reiterated in his squeakingly skinny voice.

"Yes, Henry Ford is the devil, but so is Roy now," someone spoke up.

"Well, if he's not the devil himself, then at least he's an agent of the Dark Prince, that's for sure. That's certainly verifiable. It's clearly obvious."

"Say, Cathy, why'd you ever break up with Roy?"

"Oh, I don't know, the usual reasons I suppose. That was a long time ago. A lot of little things I suppose, things that never got fixed, like always, I suppose. He definitely was dabbling in the dark magic, that's for sure. And I can see how that kind of thing could escalate and eventually affect those around him, but that's what you get when you meet guys through work, I suppose."

"You met him at work?"

"Yeah. At the dating service I worked at."

"Trolling for all the great guys, huh?"

"Yeah, pretty much."

"Did he have a nice penis?" Eddie asked, obsessed with other guy's penises, as always.

"Yeah, I suppose you could say I recall it as being alright. It was okay-looking and all, not boring or anything. It was okay."

"Like, just okay? But not necessarily nice? I heard his old friend was a little on the small side. One could say it was tiny, even. Tiny and discolored. That's what some guy told me. Yeah, some guy told me it was rather small. That's what I heard. I also heard he got fired from his job and that he did time for . . ."

"Yeah, whatever, Ed."

"Well, I heard he was in therapy."

"Therapy was invented for guys like you, Ed."

"Yeah, and I heard he had water on the brain. Yeah, that's what I heard."

"Yeah, okay, Ed."

"What about that Pete guy you were seeing there for a while. What about his wally? Did it border on the pleasant? Because I heard . . ."

"That's the funny thing about most guys. No matter what, they're always guys. They could be sitting in church, or at their mother's funeral, or watching an autopsy, or whatever—but they're always guys. They'd just be sitting there gauging how much better than everybody else they are. At least the guys my age. I hope they get better as they get older."

"Say, Cath, did you send out those birthday invitations?"

"Yep."

"Will Artis Gilmore come to my party?"

"You mean the Artis Gilmore who played center for the Kentucky Colonels of the American Basketball Association from 1971 to 1976?"

roy's the devil

"Yes, yes, that's him. He won a league title there—teaming up with Dan Issel."

"The Artis Gilmore who played for Chicago and San Antonio of the NBA. The one who finished his career with the Boston Celtics in the late 1980s? The Artis Gilmore who scored more than 22,000 points? Who grabbed more than 15,000 career rebounds? Could it be that Artis Gilmore? Huh? . . ."

"Why yes, that certainly could be the one."

"The all-time league leader in shooting percentage?"

"Yes! Yes! That's him!"

"The one with the spanking, impeccable afro? The one with the pert, razor-sharp sideburns? The one with the jaunty, chic goatee? The origin of anything and everything 'alternative'. The Source. The Origin himself. The one you turn to. The one you look to in times of crisis. The one you pray to when mired in a deep fashion funk. The One You Turn To. The One."

"Yes, of course, that's him. He's the one. All seven-foot-two of him. He's the boooosssss. He's The One."

"Thaaaaat Artis Gilmore?"

"Yes, *that* Artis Gilmore. Is he coming to my birthday party?"

"Well, I reckon he'd be mighty welcome."

"But can he make it?"

"Hasn't returned his RSVP yet."

"What about Dan Roundfield? Can Dan Roundfield make the scene? Or how about Gus Williams? I'd really like to meet Gus Williams."

"Don't know."

"Maurice Lucas? World Free? Calvin Natt? Sleepy

i'm right here

Floyd? Marques Johnson? Bob McAdoo? What about Bob McAdoo?"

"My baaaaack hurts."
"Well, stop laying on that hard concrete floor."
"It's tooo cooollld in heeeere."
"Well, get off that cold concrete floor.
"I'mmmm so boooorrrred."
"Well, stop staring at that blank wall."
"What time you pickin' us up t'night? I wanna hit that one club."
"How's eightish?"
"Eight?"
"Yeah eight."
"Yeah, eight's cool."
"Eight, you like eight?"
"Was I talkin' ta you, buster?"
"Eight's great."
"Hell, eight is enough."
"I like eight."
"Shut up. Who fuckin' cares what you like, fool."
"Eight. Yeah eight's OK, I guess."
"Eight, you like eight? That's what you like?"
"Yeah, I s'pose. Why?"
"Eight? Eight sucks."
"Eight sucks?"
"Yeah, for your information, eight just happens ta suck."
"Sucks my butt."
"Sucks yer mother."
"All night."
"My butt."

"That may be, but eight still blows. Man, where'd you grow up?"

"How can you dis eight, when eight happens to be the greatest number there is. All-time baby, all-time."

"What?"

"The number eight."

"Eight?"

"Yeah, eight."

"Eight blows. Eight blows hard, man. Real hard."

"Yeah. Eight blows wide, man."

"Seven, now there's a number."

"Yeah, seven rules."

"Seven?"

"Yeah."

"Seven sucks, man."

"Seven sucks?"

"Yeah, hate ta break it to ya, pally."

"Eight sucks more."

"You all don't know what you're talkin' 'bout. Four. Now there's a figure. Four. Solid, man. Epic. Tell yer mother. Hell, tell yer grandmother."

"Yeah, I heard that. Four rules. Four could crush seven. And you can forget eight. Eight don't even make the game. Eight. Ha. Eight can't play for ya."

"The number four rocks, man. It's a destroyer of worlds."

"No way, man. The number three is way better. The number three'll get ya high man. Any day."

"Eight, man. Eight. Eight rules over all it surveys."

A cockroach rustled under the paper on the end table next to them.

"Hey, look..." Betty pointed down to the glossy ad in her lap. "Finally, postmodern Kotex."

i'm right here

"Hey Eddie, remember when I gave you that love letter to give to that Marcy girl at work and instead of giving it to her you Xeroxed it and put it up on all the bulletin boards? And then you told her I had V.D. Remember that?"

"Hey, be cool, man."

"And remember that one time you broke into that Stacey girl's house? You know, that one girl who liked me. And you trashed her place and then told her that *I* really did it? Remember that?"

"Hey, be cool, man, I was just jokin'."

"Yeah, Eddie, you are a joke."

"Hey, that's a great jacket, by the way. And those are some awesome shoes! Hey, let me buy you a beer. No, wait, how about lunch *and* a beer?"

"Eddie, stop kissin' my ass."

"Yeah, that's a great idea . . ."

"Perhaps Roy is an agent of old Hank Ford himself. Dispatched here to spread his car culture, franchise eyesores, and anonymous strips blighting our lives and stomping out all the Mom-and-Pop stores and replacing them with alienating standardization."

"I thought I told you to shut the fuck up, you fucking geek."

"That does make sense. But clearly Roy does not possess the intelligence to apply himself to all of this. Not all by himself. Nor is he industrious enough."

"He could maybe pull off the little stuff, you know, just to get started."

"Yeah, like he could've killed my goldfish. Maybe."

"I bet he's the reason why I lost those last five jobs . . . maybe even those last four girlfriends."

roy's the devil

"Some guy told me that Roy's a baby killer, and that he has water on the brain, yeah, that's what some guy told me."

"You mean some guy you just made up, Eddie."

"I bet he's the reason I maxed out all my credit cards. That's logical."

"He was probably behind this stretch of bad weather."

"Shuuuuut the fuck up, you fucking freak."

"His mere existence would explain why my boat got repossessed . . . He probably even repossessed it himself. That's sound."

"My toaster's on the fritz—well, my favorite toaster anyway. I bet it's possessed with Roy's spirit. That's certainly a credible notion."

"He's most likely accountable for me accidentally super-gluing my eyelids together and then shooting off my left nut."

"He's probably to blame for my fear of marching band music. As well as my fear of marching-band-related paraphernalia."

"Most likely he's the reason I got my tit caught in that wringer."

"I bet he was responsible for that song 'Itchacoo park.'"

"I bet he was behind that old movie, *Wee Willy Winky*. That's sensible."

"Man, that was from way before he was even born."

"Yeah, that's my point."

"He might not've even been born. He may've been hatched, or spawned, even."

"I've always gotten a strange tingly sensation between my legs when I think of him."

i'm right here

"My feet get warm."
"Shut the fuck up, nimrod."
"I didn't say anything."
"Yeah ya did, right there."
"No I didn't."
"Yep, there ya go again, shootin' off yer smart mouth."
"Huh?"
"You gonna shut that thing or am I gonna come over there and shut that thing for ya?"
"I bet he's the reason why men are the strange, hairy mythic creatures of lore that they are . . . Yep, I bet he's behind that whole deal."
"Infernal, demonic stain!"
"No, that was your last boyfriend."
"A masher. A ruiner."
"Beelzebub! Asmodeus! Mephistopheles!"
"The Evil One!"
"The Tempter!"
"He is. He is. Yes, that makes perfect sense. He offered me a cigarette the other day."
"He offered me a malt. He ruined my diet!"
"Are we just gonna sit here and take this?!"
"What are we gonna to do about it?"
"Check him for cloven hooves!"
"Lets just kill 'im instead!"

Roy's the devil, we all agreed. And so, when he returned from the restroom, we were ready for him.

We pushed him down and took turns kicking him in the side and in the stomach.

"We gotta get all that bad shit outta you, Roy," we explained.

roy's the devil

"We'd best take care of you, before you get at us even further."

"Before you poison us with your doctrine."

"Before you impede Artis Gilmore from attending my birthday party."

"Before I tub-out again."

"It's what's best for all involved."

"You'll thank us someday."

Oddly enough, there happened to be a rake leaning up against the wall. Eddie slowly lifted it and held it over Roy. "I'm gonna pick away at you like a crusty scab." Betty picked up a large fire extinguisher and raised it above her head. I gathered some newspapers, then pulled out my lighter . . . .

"What is the nature of evil, Roy?" Betty asked, as she brought the fire extinguisher slamming down . . .

big guys in tight pants (burst in)

"Hey, make a move. Dexter, wake up, man," Carl tapped the chessboard.

I had been staring out the window. The gentle snow had covered all the cars out on the street below.

"Oh, I was just thinking. Thinking about a girl," I sighed, shaking my head, returning my attention to the game before me.

"Someone you met this weekend, eh?"

"Nooo . . ." I exhaled as I scanned the board. "I first met her in one of those narrow, maze-like back alleys of Rangoon. Usually we would exchange information among the bulrushes of the Yamuna, in New Delhi. But for some reason, that night, she preferred Rangoon."

"So . . . what about her?"

"She was beautiful. Her formulas were dizzying. The calculations filled volumes—like the peacocks blooming around us.

"One time I actually got a chance to talk to her over coffee in one of those back-alley coffee places. After chatting for awhile we decided to go up to her place. We ended up spending the night together. I woke to the hazy smell of sex.

She was lying next to me, her white, naked body entangled in the sheets on the floor. The room smelled like hot bodies on a hot day with hot mustard slathered all over them—up and down and all around. I woke with fists full of hair, and nodules and concretions all over my face—all that Rangoon coffee. They like their coffee strong there, boy.

"On the outside I was biting my lip and drooling. On the inside I was swigging whisky and shrugging, 'Yeah, why the hell not,' that little guy inside of me masturbating, thinking about a fifth grade teacher. That little angry guy within him lighting a fire. That little guy inside of the fire guy flying a kite in a grassy field, stark naked on a warm summer's day. The little guy inside of the kite guy shouting at the top of his lungs in a pornographic movie theater. The little guy inside of him dozing off at his desk at work. The little guy inside of him, an odiferous beatnik with a mommy complex and a gas can, sneaking into an open window in rural Indiana . . ."

"Yeah, so . . ." Carl interrupted.

"So, what I was thinking about was how I never saw her again."

"Never?"

"Nope."

"What happened that morning?"

"Well, like I said, the place stunk like crap—or, more accurately, like the sweat off of crap," I drew in a deep breath and looked up from the playing board. I looked out into the dark hall of my small apartment and shrugged. "The sun shone in from the louvered doors to the balcony. She was awake, curled on the floor. The sun warmed her in the bed sheet. I asked her to join me for breakfast, she agreed, climbed off the floor, stood straight, gathered herself in the bed sheet, wrapped it tightly around her, reached down and collected her skimpy clothes, took a few steps to what I assumed was the bathroom, looked back over her shoulder and smiled at me, and that was it."

"What was it?"

"That. That was it, my friend. That was the last I ever saw of her. She must have snuck out—out a window or door or something."

"What were you doing?"

"I got off the bed and wandered out onto the balcony. The wind was blowing, refreshing and cool. And when I went back in, she was gone."

"Bummer, man. Massive bummer."

"Yeah, we were all set to go out on our first date together too, to poison the city's aquifer with some anthrax . . . And now every once in a while I just go into this trance, and that's what I see. All I see is her looking over her shoulder and smiling at me. Smiling as if . . . as if she had wanted to spend the night with me for a long time, but never had the guts to do anything about it." I returned my attention to the old, worn chessboard balancing between us on the wood crate. "The last I heard she went over and burned Duncan's house down and then joined the Red Cross."

"You stuck it to her though, right? You did the do, right? Right then on her there, right?"

"Yeah, I guess we did. I remember she tasted like an old penny. But that was almost two years ago." I shook my head, "And now I doubt I'll ever taste her old pennyness again."

We had to start over. We played another game, but I found myself staring out the window again. "What is it now?" Carl begged in annoyance.

"The snow, it's just the snow—it reminds me of that firing squad. Was cold in Siberia that day, buddy boy."

"How'd you get out of that one?"

"I don't really know, I was blindfolded, leaning against the cold cinder-block wall of a building, the breeze blowing the snow into my face. It was dark all around. I could hear the militia men murmuring to themselves about thirty feet in front of my men and me, and then, 'flash,' that was it."

"What was it?"

"Someone had rescued me... It all happened so fast." I shrugged. "I heard some distant gunplay, a clap of mortar fire, a kaleidoscope of loud noises, and that was that. Like I said, I was blindfolded. It was dark. The blindfold was wrapped tightly around my head, causing difficulties with my hearing... And then someone grabbed me and the next thing I knew I was in a helicopter."

It was getting late and the snow was beginning to pile up out there. After a few more martinis, Carl had to get going.

A few nights later I was sitting in my easy chair, alone under my reading lamp, sipping a martini and flipping through an old assassin's manual of mine when I heard a strange bumping in the hall.

The bumping was slow and heavy. It sounded like a faint moaning, like a deep pit breathing in and out, like a deep pit in a field outside of Manila. Seems like I've spent too many years of my life in deep black pits in fields like that.

I felt that something out in the hall. Something strange, something unusual—some guttural wheezing, as if from a distant radiator. I got up, walked to the door, opened it and what to my surprise do I find laying out there in the hall, but some odd wormlike creature. It was long and greasy and a glistening brown—at least twelve feet in length.

i'm right here

It rolled and twisted, bumping its snout against the door, trying to get in.

"Ah, come on in you greasy wormlike thing," I said, and I held the door wider. It was five feet around its midpoint, and heavy. It inched its way in. I had to tug to help get it in. It was slow and lethargic, almost sad and lonely in its timid movement.

Over the next three weeks I fed it scraps; mopped up its constant sweaty ooze with a mop and bucket I kept behind my chair; patted its back as it lay beside me on the floor as I read at night; and kept it warm with an old blanket my grandmother had sewn.

And then one dark, snowy night some big guys in tight pants burst in. The door flew off its hinges. I jumped up, off my chair. It was immediately obvious that they wanted him. Or it.

They were decked out in suits made of black shiny rubber. They each had those tiny swimmer's goggles and black swimmer's caps on. They pushed me back. They looked very dapper, very curt and all, but obviously didn't want to get any of the thing's oozing sweat on themselves, so they donned the appropriate attire. Something natty, yet easy to hose down. I admired that, that sort of preparation.

Three of them pushed me against the wall and held me in place. I struggled as more of them came in. As I struggled, some books were knocked off my bookshelf. One of them carefully picked the books off the floor and returned them to their place on the old wooden shelf, while the others tried to drag the giant beast out. It left a trail of milky ooze as they pulled and rolled the cumbersome brown worm. My apartment was full of antiques, and they were not respectful of them. They knocked over my ornate coatrack, lamps, and end tables—an intimidation strategy that I thought quite highly of. They finally had it worked into my entryway when I heard her voice again.

I couldn't see clearly, as I had been struggling and they had their hands in my face, their black rubber gloves squeaking against my flesh, blocking my view.

"Oh, there you are, honey. Oh, look, he's hungry . . ." I heard her patting its back. Slap. Slap. Slap. "Oh, look, it's crying. You poor baby. You poor little thing, you." She drawled.

It was her. It was her. It was that girl who left me in Rangoon.

"Sorry, Dexter," she shouted. "He got away from me, the silly thing. It took forever to track him here." I could still hear her patting its back. "Are you still making up all those silly little stories for your little buddies?" I heard her stepping across the floor to me. Her high heels clacked against the wood floor. I struggled to see, but could only make out two more of the men in tight black suits. They were dragging in a silver tub of light brown slop. "Oh, so hungry. Hungry baby," she sang.

"What is that thing?" I quivered.

"Oh, sweetie, but this is our baby," she answered in baby talk, "Our baaay-beeee . . ."

adventure #25

The rain pounded the windshield as if I were driving under water, as if it were trying to get at me. The wipers couldn't brush it aside fast enough. The unmarked sedan couldn't hold back the gusts of wind. Miles of endless franchise restaurants met me—gas stations, muffler shops—an endless line on the strip leading to the abandoned airbase. All the buildings looked the same, frightening me in their familiarity. I was a thousand miles from home, in an unfamiliar rented car, but I could've been anywhere. Thus I was everywhere, everywhere at once. And yet I was nowhere.

Yuri met me out in the lost fog of a grassy field. He led me down into a dark, corrugated metal culvert, through a tunnel winding down below the base. I clutched the railing as he lead me through a labyrinth of catwalks and metal stairs that clung to the damp concrete walls above a deep, empty blackness.

Finally we reached the very bottom of the basement. Yuri swung open a heavy steel and concrete door that moved with the sound of sawing metal. My trench coat dripped pearls of rain on the cement floor, echoing down the halls in the tick tick tick of a tender clock.

adventure #25

The basement was dank and musty and full of a plantlike smell—a thick, rich dirt of a smell. But judging from the cold concrete walls and weak, yellowing bulbs, I felt as though no one had been down here in years.

Our steps echoed ahead of us—tick tick tick—around corners and splitting the darkness, the flick of the light switches rang on dryly, cracking in the air as we inched ourselves further below the installation.

After Jean-Claude escaped, we turned the building plans over to the government, then we went into hiding. I hadn't been in the country in weeks—so it was good to hear a friendly voice, a voice I could trust, a voice from the underground.

Yuri was trying to explain as we walked, our footsteps clacking ahead, falling down the concrete tunnel—traces of us—of past lives and of lives to come. He said you had to see it in order to fully understand, that it wouldn't be pleasant, but I knew I had to see. I had to find out for myself, to see if the rumors were true. If they had really kept him alive.

Things were quiet for a while as I thought, then Yuri finally spoke, "How's that thing going with you and that one girl you were tellin' me about?"

"Oh, don't ask."

"Yeah, well, don't worry about it. Things'll work themselves out. I mean we're all just a bunch of clods anyway."

I was glad he said something. It calmed me. It made things easier.

Finally, Yuri stood before the last steel door, shivering in the darkness. He told me they would kill us both if they found out what he was about to show me, his breath a fog in the cold air as he turned the key and pushed back the door

i'm right here

with a penetrating squeak that rang in my ears and touched a spark deep within me.

I drew in a breath and stepped through the door. Yuri had only opened it a crack so I had to shuffle my feet on the dusty floor to slide myself in. The room was dark, not really big, but very tall. It took a moment to adjust to the odd light, things fuzzy in the hazy background, seeming to pulsate as they came into view, getting clearer and clearer.

Yuri closed the squeaking door slowly. He left it cracked for a moment, peeking down the hall with one eye to make sure we weren't being followed. The door closed with a rumble. "Over here," he whispered and pointed behind me, leading me through the dark green fog of light. "They kept it," he whispered in a fascinated horror, as if he were afraid even to talk about it, as if it were so fantastic that he didn't believe it himself unless someone else was there to witness.

"Incredible," I uttered, the words growing in the soupy air.

A large tank came into view as we traversed the fog. It covered the entire side of the room—at least sixty feet long and fifty feet high. A heavy mechanical hum emanated from the tank and filled the air. We stood side by side, very close, as if approaching some primitive god. "He was one of those types with a peculiarly enlarged head to begin with, you'll remember," he whispered. I nodded, my mouth agape as the tank drew us closer, the gold and green liquid inside undulating clouds of haze.

"A big sloppy head, you remember—like Nixon's," he continued. Large plantlike floaties and strange bubbles roamed the tank as if they were alive. "After he died, it kept right on growing." I nodded as I listened, tingling in sick curiosity. I had to know. I just had to know. "It kept growing and growing," he continued, his voice whispering in gasps.

"They kept it to study, to talk to." Slowly I looked at him and he nodded his head as if it were all common knowledge. "It wants to record another album. A Christmas album."

Its caretakers passed in front of the floating, drowsy shape bobbing inside the tank. Some strange, heavy fluid dripped down the sides of the enlarged, lethargic head. The workers were front-lit by the eerie green light beaming from the tank, appearing as mere clouds before us, mere ghosts. They swept the floor and rubbed the tank with towels, their devoted breath exhaled cold clouds. A thick, green moss grew inside the tank and climbed to the ceiling, growing toward the door.

I winced and swallowed hard. My God, that can't be him. God help us, it can't be him. The giant head bobbed up and down slowly, like a woozy balloon. It sloshed up to the glass, mushed against it with a thundering yet muffled booooom, the reverberation echoing in my chest like a drum.

Emerging from the fog of the dark, murky liquid, Elvis's engorged, bloated head nudged the glass again with a slow, weak, echoing booooooooommm. I jumped back as its heavy tone surrounded us, filling my chest again—as if he were inside of me, fighting to get out.

"He's about twenty feet in diameter." Yuri swallowed as Elvis's large, sad eyes slowly opened, as if from a deep sleep. The long raggy hairs of his mutton-chop sideburns swirled freely. They seemed to be weeds at his side, wiggling away from his pale face, his eyes half open in a deep, old sadness.

"Due to the magnitude of his brain, Elvis is now a clairvoyant, although many feel he has always had the gift."

"Amazing," I whispered to myself.

"He helps us out with problems from time to time, but the last few years he's mostly kept to himself," Yuri shrugged

i'm right here

as if there was nothing that could be done. "His telepathic powers are a wonder, yet he remains bored, or at least unimpressed with them. His telekinetic abilities offer him no comfort or bemusement."

Sympathy rushed over me. I felt it filling the room, pushing the walls out further and further. I wanted to do something, I *needed* to do something.

"Go ahead . . ." Yuri said shrugging as if reading my thoughts. And I stepped up to it, gradually, one slow, deliberate step at a time. I raised my hand and put it up to the glass, holding it in the air for a second before placing it on the clammy tank, in front of his gigantic chin.

I closed my eyes, as if praying it weren't true, the thought kicking at me, kicking at my sides until my tongue swelled up and I choked out the hard air. I felt I should pull the plug, let him fade on with dignity.

Where's the humanity? A deep voice whispered inside of me as those giant, sad eyes bored into me, his jowly cheeks vibrating in the cloudy fluid.

"He grows at something like a millimeter a day," Yuri informed as he stepped to the tank. "Why?" I exhaled in disbelief, my hand squeaking down the condensation on the glass. But Yuri offered no answer, no consolation, as if to say it-is-as-it-is, his silence cementing it all.

A technician in a white lab coat approached the tank, looking down at the floor as he mopped. He looked up and offered a half-smile and a nod of affirmation to the giant King. He fumbled with the mop handle, rolling it around in his palm like an offering to a great mythic creature whose consciousness is as vast as the universe.

I watched his technicians, his faithful rednecks with their pointed mutton-chop sideburns and greasy slicked back hair. I reached to the glass for support. "This doesn't seem

adventure #25

right," I shook my head, closed my eyes and pushed my other palm up to the tank. "This doesn't seem right at all," I mouthed, trying to push it all away.

"We're just supposed to let him die then? Is that it?" He exhaled.

"This just isn't fair . . . to use him like this. It isn't right." I shook my head as we stepped back, away from the murky tank.

"Look, I'm not responsible. That's why we need your help. We want to put him to rest—to put our past to rest."

"Well then show me the guy who is."

"He'll be difficult to find, but if we let it out right he may just come looking for *us*."

"So I'm the bait, then, is that it?"

"Emm, something like that," he nodded over to the tank.

Suddenly a bright, crisp "ping" cut the air. Our heads snapped to the metal door. The knob jiggled. The door slowly began to open . . . and Yuri grabbed my arm and whispered, "Oh my . . ."

who's going to sing country western to the urban underprivileged?

Part 1

I had been living on Dewy's couch for about a month when I finally met his roommate, Shelly-Pete Oh-my-gosh. Not to be narrow-minded or judgmental, but his face was far too big for his eyes. His eyes were like a raisin and a fly in an enormous bowl of oatmeal. Then again, I didn't have my glasses on at the time.

His belly hung out over his belt like a big, happy target—smiling at me, tempting me. I wanted to confront it, jiggle it, rub it, sing a song to it, whisper sweet nothings to it, compliment it—the works. A tempting target indeed, but useless to our cause. I watched as he lurched around, his arms growing ten feet long and longer, and then suddenly receding just as fast—until I put on my glasses.

Immediately, I liked the guy.

Dewy, the grade school principal, was slumped in one of the many couches. He stared up at the ceiling in his rabbit suit. I was sprawled on another couch across the room. Dewy also had on a cowboy hat, cowboy boots with jangling cowboy spurs, cowboy chaps with fringe, and a set of six guns in corresponding holsters. "I wanted to be a rabbit," he said softly. His soggy words sagged under their saturated utterance. "I also wanted to be a cowboy. So I'm a cow-rabbit... or, er... a rabbit-boy." He searched the ceiling for the answer with a "why can't I be both?" face.

His arms were distended. He was in a turgid state. He sucked the barrel of his freshly painted pink shotgun. He had it propped up in his lap, squeezing it between his legs to hold it in place. The worried expression of burden was cast into his face like a porcelain plate. The night before, his father had shaved his body and mowed all the neighbors' lawns while nude. He carried his hair in a shoebox and had the words *worry, worry, worry, burden, coffee,* and *burger* written all over his naked body with a laundry marker. Grass clippings stuck to his sweaty body as he glistened deep into the hot night. When the cops finally cornered him, he made his escape by diving through a hedge and then climbing a garage. He was seen the next morning at a strip mall several miles away. It was reported that he had pasted his hair all over his body with Elmer's school glue.

The phone rang. It startled Dewy to the point of him jumping, jostling his limp thumb in the trigger, and discharging the shotgun—almost rocketing his tired brains to splatter across the galaxy of ceiling. A brief expression of relief swelled across his pale, stiff face. His eyes fluttered, floating dreamily up to the ceiling as if picturing his pink, fluffy think-matter clinging to the pasty gray ceiling—like young clouds, blushing with innocence.

The tingly, warm scent of gunpowder watered my eyes. The sweet, harmonic sounds of the blast vibrated my groin, tickling me and making me giggle.

Part 2
(The Lost Chapter of *The Bridges of Madison County*)

Flickering specks of morning dripped through the drapes to calm the murky ceiling, to enlighten the gentle, gray mist of shotgun blast, thin strands of black smoke, creamy clouds of billowing plaster.

The sky winked through the hole in the ceiling. And Dewy, relieved, smiled up as he sank back into the couch.

I had urged Dewy to rejoin his old band. It was good for him to have the creative outlet, to be able to share a piece of himself with others. But "Electrologist," Uganda's most cheerfully blithe death-rock band had gone on the road without him and were now missing.

I had always admired him and his father. Two of the few sane men I've ever met. Recent events only proved to broaden the sentiment beyond my puny imagination. I knew he was going to be OK now. I knew his father would write, to remain connected to his chosen society, as he eluded the ominous stranglehold of such an obsolete, arbitrary culture—leaping from that sinking rat ship, proudly wearing his freedom like a veritable gas mask against the leaking, pungent mixture of others' illusions and expectations.

The pride I felt in them compelled me to get up and face the day. I coughed from the smoky clouds of plaster and thrust myself into the hall and proudly trotted down the musty stairs of the old house.

Once outside, I stood on the sidewalk, surveying the morning with dignity and self-respect. I stood in my flannel pajamas, the ones with the lead pipes imprinted all over them. I took in the bright morning—the blue sky, the fluffy white clouds, the winos, the drug dealers, the burned-out cars, the piles of old tires, the heartbroken teenagers, the *who's going to sing country western*

moping existentialists—and realized my car was gone, towed, yet again, without due authority. The city always seems to assume that it's abandoned. Ah, my gold Pinto, my den, my only possession—held together by rust. All but undrivable. My sanctuary of contemplative introspection.

(Ordinarily, something like a string of unusually long fire trucks would be blocking it in anyway—or unimaginably enormous dump trucks—anything to further amplify my own ineffectualness.)

I stood in the morning's misty breath and recognized some acquaintances approaching from up the block. It was Jonny Um and Becky Toilet-plunger and Betty My-back-is-killing-me and Davey Washes-his-hands-a-lot.

"Wanna hit a stop-and-rob for some doughnuts?" Becky called across the narrow street from under the trees.

"No, no, not that you stupid idiot. Let's go do something. That's it, we're goin' fishin'!" Jonny bossed.

"Um, no, fish don't like me," I shouted back. "Like most things, they labor intently to stay away from me. Fishing is a lie to me. But thanks for askin'."

Jonny, the billboard salesman, seemed to become cross with me. "I know a great little stream out by Interstate Golgotha. We just put some billboards up there last week. Come on, we're all gonna go work out afterward!"

"Umm, no . . . no, thank you—I like you folks and all, but I gotta do some stuff. You know how it is." I shrugged.

"You're not very achievement-oriented, are you?" he stepped off the curb in his dashing new suit made from elephant skin, the latest in formal business attire.

"Depends on what you consider an achievement." I shrugged. "I gotta put in some time in the community garden out back." I tilted my head in the direction of the back alley. "You know, 'Live free or die' and all."

"Well, we're goin' fishin', then we're gonna work out some, then we're gonna go out an' tell a buncha shitty lies aboutcha. 'K?" He looked at me like he needed to be nice to someone at that moment, but just couldn't figure out how.

"I look forward to hearing about them." I shrugged as they lazily approached from across the street. (Eventually a compromise was reached. They would only spread filthy lies about me on Tuesdays—jazzy lies, replete with improvisation: pedophile, pedophile, arsonist... racist, klepto, klepto, klepto.) Their tiny lies were little magic locks. And years later, all the people would remember were all those locks that had me hidden away in a high prison tower that only a good woman could rescue me from. Their lies were like sadness, and Shelly-Pete and Dewy were the magic that was dispatched to foil the sadness.

"We tried wooing you nicely, now you're comin' with us," one of them mumbled as they picked me up and lifted me thoughtfully above their heads. I raised my arms as I swayed this way and that, trying to reach and balance as they spun me around and bobbed me along. Each one gripped a leg of mine, their arms wrapped tightly around me. Someone raised a doughnut up to me and another blast barked from upstairs—*ka-boom*—and behind me tiny holes splintered away pieces of the siding upstairs. And I giggled some more as I struggled to balance.

what I did last night

There was this letter that I was going to write to you about a story that I was thinking about writing about a guy who I don't know yet who goes over to visit this other guy, like people tend to do on occasion, but that guy isn't home so he walked back home when he saw a middle-aged woman standing off to the side with tired hair like an old field, and looked as if she had never had a kind word spoken in her direction. I stirred the beans and got naked. You're lost on the bus. Nothing looks familiar. Now you're driving the bus, a malodorous fetidness about. A fetor. A mephitis as we passed the glue factory.
    a noctambulant apparatus
    an incubating contrivance
    a device of unusual configuration
    a pulchritudinous conflagration
    an indignant confabulation
    a disagreeable odor from the rendering plant
    I'm forty three years old, but I have the look about me that a five-year old would have, which is ok by me. Now we're sitting on the bus together. It's shaking us violently as we speed down the railroad track, a coal train bearing down, it's

i'm right here

headlight shining down into the bus, down the aisle, blinding us as we laugh, you with a toaster in your lap, me spraying oven cleaner in my hair, burning my eyes, stinging my throat, fantasizing about masturbation, my big toe complaining about the weather. "I've failed you!" I scream, and the night crashes down all around us.

Lying in the smoldering ashes in a grassy ditch in the morning, entangled in the rusty barbed wire of an old fence, clouds oozing by in the bloodshot sky, blushing blue to pink, I begin to see it all more clearly now. I think I'm finally beginning to understand things. I see it all more clearly. My legs are numb. I can't move. I see it clearly. I loved you.

male nude reclining

There was this rambling thirty-page letter that I was going to write to you concerning the grandeur and lore of Jan Brady's breasts (a "fan letter," as I called it), but I got caught up in that cooking/ballroom dance/furniture stripping class.

The professor held up his wrist, leaned over, and said to a young woman, "I got this watch because you liked it, and thus I thought you might like me." And I was thinking, "Yeah, right—poke 'er once for me, Doc."

Bigbee was cleaning fish in the back. He had always worn two pairs of underwear (just in case he got in an accident and they would have to take him to the hospital) but lately his groin has bulged with the electrodes hooked up to his privates, so as to share the glorious experience of childbirth with his wife.

There was this bucket sitting on the floor in the corner of the empty cabin. The cabin had been built by the stocky women of the valley as a public works project in the 1930s and Dotty—the smelliest of them— why Dotty, doggoneit, well she just upped and fabricated that bucket one rainy morning as a love letter to another angry and stubborn immigrant who grew up in a valley that . . .

...the yellow door... the cow in the hall... the man in the tree... the bucket was red. It was full of water. Dotty had lied. She had run out and stolen the bucket and now, years later, sensing this, my heart was breaking over the affair. I couldn't even pull on my tights.

The Shaker community was in ruins as word of the bucket seeped out. Entire bucket cults committed mass suicide. Personally, I was so disturbed that I began attacking one of the ritualistic floor scrubbers who kept a 24-hour scrubbing vigil in the cabin.

"You're crazy!" They doubted my theory.

"Crazy like a well-oiled machine," I tapped a finger to my gourd, my noodle, my melon, and held my torch a little higher.

The flat, gray metal sky rippled shyly. And I watched the clouds turn in the water of the bog as I lay naked in the tall weeds, flicking the lint from my navel and listening to my secret Chet Baker recordings: "The Tears of the Disappointed Womb," and "The Maidenhead," and "The Mount of Venus."

And I dreamt of an art gallery, glorious and radiant; imagined a painting of a guy sitting on a curb, eating food out of the gutter, looking up just in time to catch some girls approaching from across the street. He has a pathetic crush on one of them. A big sloppy crush. Yet does not know what to do about it, never getting a fair chance to implement his feelings, never getting a fair chance to act on them, to unroll them, like a beautiful rug.

And I imagined a painting of a man sitting in the window of the cabin of a great silver zeppelin, floating alone in the midnight fog—his arm sticking out, feeling the clouds, another man tied to a chair in the corner of the dimly lit room.

And I imagined a painting of a husband and wife in their kitchen; he's got a flamethrower strapped to his back, and they're embracing one another. They're both looking out the window at a monkey in a tree in their backyard.

And I imagined a painting of a man looking out the window of the attic of a small house in the middle of the night. He's wearing a mangy cat costume and holding an old stuffed duck in his arms.

And I imagined a painting of a lady in an easy chair reading at night in the small living room of her tiny apartment. A giant likeness of her peers in through the windows. Atop the building across the street sits a great billboard with her smiling face on it. It looms over her as she slowly turns the pages.

And I imagined a painting of a man lying in a smoldering ditch, entangled in an old fence, the sun slowly rising, realizing too late that he's in love. I guess sometimes you have to go through some pretty sticky shit to attain clarity.

And I imagined a painting of a man running up a narrow street, scurrying after the girl he loves. Sometimes life is just that basic. Sometimes life seems to come down to those tiny little moments—moments so small that you hardly notice them as they pass you by. Moments you barely notice until it's all too late. It's so sad sometimes that life is just that simple, that fragile.

And I watched the clouds in the water of the bog as I lay swatting flies in the tall weeds, my body glorious and radiant. And I thought, "What happened? Why all of this?" But the clouds didn't know. The sun didn't know. And the wind didn't know. And gradually, I began to expose my life for the cowardly, ass-kissing sham that it had become.

thirty seven

self portrait

I answered the phone with a slow, gravelly, "hellllllloooooo." Normally I don't mind getting calls in the middle of the night. Hell, I'd talk to anyone—even someone who hates my guts. Even someone who wants very bad that I cease to exist. But this was an unnatural situation in that I had been experiencing an unusually unfortunate week and was thus very very run down, and therefore not at my best—and certainly not at my best middle-of-the-night-conversation-wise.

There was angry breathing on the other end.

"Hello, who's there?" My voice was weak.

The breathing quickened.

"Look, I'm going to have to disconnect you if you insist upon being impolite. Who is there please."

"Someone ... [hot, angry breathing] ... Someone who hates your guts."

"Well how about that. Is there anything specific on your mind that you would like to talk about?"

"No."

thirty seven

"Well, what exactly are you angered by, something I said or did, or perhaps something I didn't say or forgot to do—an oversight on my part perhaps? What in particular do you dislike about me per se?"

"Yooouur guts." His manner of speech was deliberate—slow and slurred.

"Hmmm, do you care to elaborate? Anything else you would like to add or get off your chest, anything else you dislike about me? Please, feel free to speak openly."

"Mmm, no. Just your guts . . . Oh, wait—that and the fact that you fucking talk too much."

"Ah, well that's good—that's a good start, you'll feel better about opening up and getting that off your mind. Ah, anything else—please, continue."

"You fucking talk too much . . ." The voice trailed off like there was something else there.

"And?"

"*And* you don't really fucking say anything. It's all just superficial wrapping—blah blah blah, endlessly. I fucking hate that."

"Yes, that can be rather tedious."

"Fucking drives me ta drink."

"Hmmm. Are you drinking now?"

"No, but I sure feel like it."

"Well it's rather late; what *are* you doing? Not that it's any of my business."

"You bet your worthless ass it ain't any a yer bizness."

Silence.

"OK."

"Well. . . if you're gonna be all nosy and get all personal—I just got home from the bar and on the way I ran a red light an now I'm gonna call the cops an report myself—tell 'em what I did."

"Yeah, that's a good idea."

"So I gotta go. Good night, sleep well . . . Oh yeah, one more thing—I've got your side."

"My what?"

"Mmm, your side. Yep, it looks like I got just about all a it in here. I'm the one who's got it. That's all. I just thought you should know."

Then whoever it was hung up. I had no idea what he was mumbling about. But then the next morning, leaving for work, I pulled out of the garage and noticed it. I sat there in the drive and stared ahead. All the siding on my house was gone. The tar paper flapped in the morning breeze—like a kid's hand out the bus window, waving to mother on the first day of school.

the escape

They must've slipped me a mickey. I'm lying on the floor in my best pin-striped suit, in blissful slumber as a tiny steamroller slowly approaches. I'm awakened in horror by its heavy humming. I roll over—the damn thing is inches from my ear.

Slowly I reach and lift it. It's very heavy and dense. About the size of a shoe. The little driver is wearing light blue coveralls and a bright orange hard hat. I study him carefully.

In bewildered anger I shake him off his little black chair.

He hangs, dangling, clutching his little black knobs and staring down at the floor below.

Confusion, terror, panic take hold. I shake him loose, like a bug.

thirty seven

The room is empty: 1. several doors, 2. white walls, 3. golden hardwood floors, 4. painted white trim, 5. ornate light fixture, 6. no light switch.
I pull myself closer as he lies sprawled on the floor. 1. The awe, the wonder of it all. 2. What is the meaning of this? 3. Why me?
He is coming to, shaking his little head and trying to pull himself up. I pinch him between my two fingers and lift him to my now giant face. "Who sent you?!!!" I scream. "Who sent you?" I sob beggingly.
1. Tell me. 2. Or else. 3. The tongue, it stirs.
I lift him to my mouth. Little muffled cries as I slip him in, between my tightly puckered lips.
He wiggles and slides out and falls. I reach, but he bounces and squirms and rolls himself off my frantic palm. He tumbles through the air. Free fall.
He hits the floor, rolls, scrambles to a crawl. Before I know it he's headed for a door.
I'm after him, crawling across the floor, but he dives and slides under the door. I recoil back, as if the door itself were poison. I slide myself back to the middle of the room. I feel bigger now, giant-like. The light goes off. It must be time to sleep. Maybe if I lie back down it'll all go away.
I return my head to the golden wood floor. I clutch the steamroller and pull it close to me, nestling it in my bosom. I feel its hard metal, its heaviness, its truth, its honesty. I close my eyes. Hell, I need the rest anyway.

toothbrush

[*Gazing into the medicine cabinet*] "Can I move your moist toothbrush over one-fourth of an inch?"

i'm right here

[*Lying on the divan*] "No . . . [*sipping wine*] . . . you cannot."

"But . . . but why?"

"Because it is my toothbrush and I'd rather not have it moved. Can you respect that? It's mine, I picked it out, and it is, in a sense, a part of me, an extension of self. So don't touch it, don't look at it, don't even think about it."

"You should be flattered that I would want to touch your toothbrush—or anything of yours for that matter, that I would want to reach out to you, to touch a part of you, something so personal, so delicate and intimate. That shows the ultimate in respect—that I would want to touch a part of you."

[*exasperated*] "Oh, I knew you'd say something like that . . . No. There is, after all, no respect there because I asked you to please not touch it. Now leave it be. And that is the end of that."

"I didn't realize you felt so strongly about it; it's just that there are these two very large African hissing cockroaches mounting and humping it."

"Oh . . . well in that case, please feel free to move it one-fourth of an inch. And thank you for asking . . . [*lighting cigarette*] . . . and say, do you recall that rainy weekend on the beach in Bermuda, when you ate that bad papaya and your testicles turned a ripe red and each swelled to the size of grapefruit?"

"Our second date—wearing that skimpy yellow Speedo—yow! Almost as romantic as our first—Embers. I tried impressing you by pistol-whipping the manager, and you, why you reciprocated by mooning the terrified patrons. I never told you, my little radish, but I was so proud."

untitled / funky drummer

"I'm lonely."

"I'm lonely too."

"Well, let's do something. Let's go shopping."

"That's not doing something."

"Sure it is."

"Is not."

"Is too."

"I don't have anything to go shopping for. And neither do you."

"Yeah I do. I need a new couch. A good sex-couch. A couch that really kicks ass."

"I'm not in the mood to look at couches, ass-kickin' sex-couches or not."

"Well, we can just walk around then."

"Mmm, I don't know. When we go shopping we always only end up where you want to go. Besides, I hate shopping; it's a boring waste of time and no fun. Also, we always just end up back here and in bed, so when you say 'let's go shopping,' I know you really only mean 'Let's have sex.'"

"No, I really only mean 'I want to do something with you,' shopping being just one option. . . . How 'bout a movie?"

"Mmm, no. Same thing."

"How 'bout goin' out ta eat then?"

i'm right here

"Mmm, no. Again, we always only end up where you want to go. Why don't you go to your boxing class?"

"Nah, I got kicked outta it for fighting, I'm hurtin' for a dog. A hot dog, that is."

"That's very Freudian."

"I'm a hot-dog whore. I admit to that. It's been an issue with me for a long time. Hmm, what about a lecture at the university?"

"I can't understand half those people . . ."

"Yeah, I know, 'The didactic idiom of the metaphor . . .'"

" 'Is refracted through . . . the space-time continuum . . . yabba-dabba-doo.' "

"And hey, sex with me was mind-shattering. . . Transcendent."

"Yeah, all guys say stuff like that."

"Like two drunk, horny sailors out on leave. Two drunk sailors, baby. Two sailors."

"Ah huh."

"Hmm, I'm runnin' outta ideas here. Seems I been sellin' insurance so long I can't even make the simplest decision on my own. Ah, how 'bout comin' over for a bite?"

"That sounds nice, but once more, we always only end up in bed together, due to the loneliness."

"You're saying you're not attracted to me, little spifferino?"

"Yes, in fact that is precisely what I am saying, in that way, but not in a friend kind of way—because you're kind of unsupportive . . . and bossy. . . Oh yeah—and you complain a lot."

"Am not, you little spunkrag."

"And we always end up in these horrible disagreements, and I'm getting too old for that, you unfathomable moron."

thirty seven

"We do *not* disagree a lot, you twitchy little bastard."
"We do too, little ass-breath."

(Cockroaches danced in his cupboards, on plates and dry goods. At first bunches of them jitterbugged on the butter—reefer fiends one and all. Then the lindy in the flour, mmm, mmm. And finally, as it got late, they settled into romantic waltzes. After which they went home and copulated while the younguns skanked to the Circle Jerks' *Group Sex* album, and the face of Jesus appeared as a rust mark on his old washing machine—out back on the tilting, weed infested porch in this reeking, backwoods hick town, as two CEOs from Proctor & Gamble defrosted his freezer with screwdrivers, and dreamt of better days.)

"OK, well if that's how you're gonna be, then I'm gonna go out into the backyard and climb into an oil drum and stare up at the sun."
"Yeah, well, that's fine, you just do that! I'm just goin' down and hide in the basement . . . and type away on my novel while chewing on my old shoes."

(To overcompensate for the intense brightness, flaps of skin slowly evolve over his eyes, developing mere pinholes, his eyes becoming two pores in a sea of face, his flesh solidifying to a leather-hard cardboard.)

(The darkness causes her eyes to form together, casting a large cycloptic eye in the center of her pasty gray face. Her bent-over posture solidifies into a crab-like ectoskeleton, and her hands grow into claw-like key punchers.)
(It's funny, the things we turn into, each seemingly content in our own myopia, as small gray creatures file into

a long string of city busses in a clearing near the woods at the edge of town, and the drummer out in the garage begins to get funky.)

april 6th
(our world became a blinding white void)

I'm ironing some pants when I hear the neighbor outside the window. The neighbor, Dan Pastorini, a former quarterback for the Houston Oilers in the golden 1970s, is peeking in the window like a child. I notice him, but don't let on that he's been found out. (I'd heard his go-cart pull into the mud of the flower bed outside.)

Lately he has been sneaking around with a flashlight. He crouches in the bushes outside my bedroom window and shines it onto the ceiling while I lay in bed trying to sleep. He'll whip it around and around in circles, trying to distract me, trying to psych me out. I have to chase him away with a broom, running down the street in the clammy, dank night, the trees hanging over us like a tunnel. Occasionally I have to yell out to the world with a bullhorn, or call his parents long distance even.

After a while he starts showing up with two flashlights, one in each eager hand. "Stop it!" I shout. "Stop it!!" I demand, lying in bed, deep into the night as the lights circle above me, dancing on the ceiling and walls. "Ssssssstooooop iiiiiiiit!!" I plead. "Ssssssssstoooooooop iiiiiiit," I sob.

I hear him now, sifting around in the bushes. I hear something rattle.

He gives the signal and someone flips a switch. Evidently there are these giant circus spotlights positioned outside of every window. Very clever. Very clever indeed. The insides of our little house suddenly jump with blinding light and our world becomes a blinding white void.

As I iron in the blinding white void I wonder what things will happen to me, and what I'll be like when I'm thirty seven.

And I think to myself that there's nothing better in all of creation than ironing some pants at 11:35 on a Wednesday night while Lori sits in her silky black underwear doing her nails on my bed as the Twins lead Seattle 5 to 4 in the sixth and the spring breeze calms my arms with its cool breath and all of its dreams of the months to come.

let's wrestle!

I was having dinner with scott baio when I saw her again

The sweet, punching stench of materialism blew around like a soggy belch from another long night, from deep out of another uncommonly dark tickle club. Bugs wiggled under the burden of that potential. I could feel them all, as if just under my skin—a moment of anticipation as I sat in the air terminal, sucking grasshoppers from a baby food jar. An impatient Scott Baio fidgeted and paced.

Scott was hungry too. He wanted to get some burritos, wondering who could produce the largest bowel movement. Unfortunately he was very competitive in those petty, scientific ways in which men can be at times.

And that's when I saw her. An old friend from proctology school. She was standing in a checkout line. The enormous white terminal breathed around her. She wore its bright light as a lacy halo in the blue night.

Until that moment it seemed that everything that mattered had already happened. The secret war in Antarctica had irrevocably changed me. The stink from my body cast was humiliating—a reminder of being left out there, having to hitchhike back—just another bad breakup, I guess. As if it mattered.

i'm right here

And then, suddenly, there she was. That's how these things happen, though—just suddenly, they're in front of you.

There she was.
I wanted to be with her. I wanted to be around her. I was drawn to her—drawn to her curving butt, to her roast-beef ears, her gravel-pit elbows, her fuzzy knuckles, her below-average dental work, her abnormally hairy back, her freakishly large calves. Imperfections so eternal they could make you cry. I was drawn to her like a child's painting to a refrigerator. I belonged with those calves, thick glistening white appliances. I deserved them. My emotional want list was agape. That back! A daunting task to be sure. However, one which would provide a challenging and mind-stimulating hobby of problem-solving skills for years to come. Those ears. Give me a girl with big ears—big ol' flappers hangin' out there. I'm an ear-man, after all. And her name ringing out in her meaty Polish accent—Annelida Hirudinea! Annelida Hirudinea! To conquer her hermaphroditic heart would be to conquer the very sky.

Even just being near her I felt that life was complete—that there was finally some sort of meaning to it all, that maybe I could finally decipher and understand it.

Unfortunately a strange man sat between us on the plane, despite my bribe of a dozen German U-boats to the booking agent.
        he wore a painfully clever handlebar mustache
his gangrenous words, like a lit fuse
                his soggy face
   his twentieth century mocked me

I was having dinner with scott baio

        his modernism
            his mushroom-cloud eyes pleaded with me
his rusty-hinge voice made me want to sell used cars in Akron, Ohio
    his freight train sighs like a redneck reloading
               his six lane religions
        his eyes a grease fire in a drive-in on the edge of town
    his old wig, like a house on fire, caused my tapeworm to
stir in my lower intestine
          his lips, like nipples growing all over my butt
      his pedantic pamphleteer pantheism made me want to
grow a giant afro
       his epochal gusts made me want to open a driving school
  his wheezing breath like a shopping cart tied to a station wagon
    his dark alley eyes receding into their ditch-like trenches
            like a rocket taking off
  his toothless grin made me want to have relations with a close
relative then gouge my own eyes out with my thumbs
        his obsequiousness made me want to shoot myself
           out of a cannon
    his snobbery made me want to dress up like the mayor's
wife, then follow her around town
      his soft forehead caused me to do a cowardly little jig
              in my mind
his promiscuous hair made me want to kill a wild boar with my
bare hands.

    From this distance the pine trees hugged the woolblanket mountain like a secret library. Bad middle names stared me in the face as we flew over, amplifying everything sour in life, causing me to fidget with further discomfort. I began considering all the lousy things: all the times a girl told me she never wanted to see me again—all the times a boss said they never wanted to see me again—all the times a host bade me farewell while holding a propane torch to my face.

i'm right here

Watching *Rat Patrol* on my sneaky little TV didn't help like it used to—even with the volume secretively mumbling its tiny, vague whisper.

My feet were burning. I wanted to pick away at the fungus, but the advanced case of gout I was fighting had my hands locked up like two claws. I was loaded, baby—constant painful erections; irritable bowel syndrome; transitory episodes of one-eyed blindness. Yep, I had it all goin' for me.

I put my hand down my throat. I acted as if to be on the verge of vomiting, and thus got to sit by her—a wise move. The strange man slid over; he was sporting an old pin-striped suit, hot pink with thin glittery stripes. He mentioned his ranch as we flew over—a mere forty feet above the rolling grassy fields, herds of elephants, the down-spouts of the hot-pink two-story sparkling with silvery glitter.

The sun danced off his indigo lake like a cliché of America—winking and twinkling at me. She shared some of her delicate end-of-the-world scenarios. And offered some of her corrosive assassination theories (chafing, burning, and raw). They sawed right through me—a valuable weapon to be sure. "Jackie paid Lee Harvey because of his cheating." She chewed her sautéed condor and gazed out the window. "That's what I woulda done."

"Sure. Sure. Of course he did. Absolutely." I nodded attentively.

A pleasant surprise as we walked down into the bomb bay and the crew was sitting around watching TV. "What are you doing down here?" "Oh, just watchin' an old tape of you two making love." Unfortunately, they seemed bored.

She began cleaning her furniture with Brut cologne—and sneaking sips. I used the Pledge for hairspray—and looked presentable, with a lustrous sheen and a lemony fresh

scent. I guess the best you can do sometimes is just to graciously accept what the day can offer.
We made out in the rear gun turret. She wore her sexy monocle and Jackson Pollock underwear. I wore my cologne, Musty Brewery. Blood flooded out of my cranium to settle down into my groin, rendering me light-headed and utterly defenseless against her soothing metaphors. We pulled the levers and dropped the payload, bombing a herd of unsuspecting elephants from above. Damn elephants. Through the bomb bay doors we watched them disappear into the soft cottony clouds of churning brown smoke and earth.

Her sexual sophistication caused me to go into seizures—legs twitching, head snapping, arms flailing—the best ten seconds of my life. Upon climaxing I immediately slipped into a mild coma, as usual. Hours later I came to, finding myself crawling down the aisle. Groggy. My lower extremities tingling and heavy, like dragging bags of wet cement. She turned to me and whispered, "You're the king," like I always beg her to when we've finished coupling. Then she returned to relaxing with the latest issues of *Ferret World, Modern Ferret, Progressive Ferret,* and the like.

We were married the next day.

Hedgehogs and woodchucks served as maids of honor and best men. We ate them at the reception, in the outhouse behind the tilting old barn, funhouse mirrors everywhere, a path of mud puddles, boiled cabbage, and candles as far as my good eye could see. Scott stewed in the corner. The three of us honeymooned in the backyard—in one of my deep black pits—each wearing clothes ripped beyond recognition. I was certain the "castaway look" was set to make a big comeback.

i'm right here

The next day we noticed some teenagers wandering off with the giant parade balloon of us making love. It was entitled "The Happy Time." So we snuck into the neighbor's backyard and tiptoed off with *their* rigid zeppelin airship. It was shaped to the form of them making love. It was entitled "The Kaiser." We tiptoed it down the block, the wind clinging to our paperbag pajamas, pebbles sticking to our feet. We giggled in the gray mist of dawn and set the airship free in a grassy field. It should be free, we reasoned.

And when we got back, the delivery people had positioned my wedding present to her in the front yard, despite the injunction from the neighbors—a stunning life-size bronze statue of two muscular horses mating, one mounting the other with a grammar school pledge-of-allegiance sentimentality. (She always had possessed a sophisticated appreciation for equestrian statuary.)

Later that day, she left me—mentioning briefly in her note scratched onto the wall with a coathanger, that it had been a real "gas," but that she was unprepared for such a serious relationship, and indicating the pungent odor of hedgehog fecal matter was further pushing her away. But they all seem to say that, don't they.

I stood and watched the sun set in a rolling field of golden grass. I adjusted my loin cloth. I held a petri dish and couldn't help thinking how wonderful it all was. I knew if I could just talk to her, we could work things out. I could hose down the hogs, maybe get a bigger shack.

I felt like climbing a metal ladder and grabbing onto a power line. I felt like eating 150 bananas. I felt like taking a pottery class.

The long grass blew around my legs in a soft whisper of wind. The fumes from the decomposing elephants were overwhelming. Standing there in that yellow-and-pink haze of setting sun, I couldn't help feeling like one of those child actors who grows into their teens on the show—growing up before the world, from a cutie-pie into a grotesque loping gigantoid, towering awkwardly above the other actors, with enormous features monstrously distorted beyond imagination. Oh, to be so full of luck. Of all my beautiful imperfections, why couldn't I be blessed with a lovely thyroid condition?

She met up with another gentleman at the bus station. His résumé indicated he was a zookeeper who had abandoned his post. He had twelve hard years of pirate experience—mostly in the Caribbean. I was busy exploring all the dynamic complexities of toast. Me and the hogs crawled into my last U-boat, to get away for a while. I kept her toothbrush in the medicine cabinet, hoping she would return. And every time the godforsaken phone rang, I prayed that it was her.

Impatient, Scott sat in the back, baking us a cake and sporting one of his impressive pro-wrestling masks. "Let's get the gang back together! Come on, let's go after Robby Benson! Let's track him down like a dog!" he urged.
With the aid of a little goodold-fashioned peer pressure, he dyed his hair a wonderful platinum blond. Several weeks ago my posse of incontinent midget wrestlers had thrown a blanket over Scott's iconoclastic head. They housed him warmly in a small closet and clothed him in leather belt-like straps. After several days, he asked to join us. I was concerned about him—and who isn't, after all. I needed to know that he was in good hands. And that's how I felt about her. So I dispatched the legions of little diapered grapplers,

i'm right here

sprinkling them across the land like hairy, leaking hopes—out across the land to plead for her return.

They climbed into their enormous cars—Cadillacs, Lincolns, dump trucks, cement mixers. With the help of the Pig Man, the bickering albino hermaphrodite Siamese dwarfs (Petey and Sloan) finally traced her to Europe. But she gave them the slip, first disabling Petey and Sloan by knocking their heads together like coconuts, then disguising herself as an Amway salesman.

The zookeeper took her up in his triplane, but something had gone terribly wrong. She reached for his hand, in that blood-red flying machine, now shredded beyond recognition, as he crawled through the stinging weeds. "Hi, how ya doin', hello. I bet if we drove really fast we could probably make that movie," she reassured him as she polished her ax.

"Death, yeah, well, it won't get me ..." He stared up at her gallantly, sputtering as she caressed his forehead, his head resting in her lap. "... I'm goin' out with some panache—something people will remember, something world-class, something they'll be talking about for a good long time, something they'll lay in bed at night and think about, something cool and really old world, like a car bomb or a stampeding goat herd or getting eaten by a hippo, digested even, or rolled over by a steamroller. Yeah, I want to go out with some dignity."

The memory of her slowly gets misplaced in the blowing fields of golden wheat and waving green grass. Her smile joins the ghostly dreams of the wind. Her ankles become the ancient white whispers of the clouds. Her touch becomes the infinity of a rippling creek. Her hairy back becomes the blue of the Saturday afternoon sky.

I was having dinner with scott baio

Scott puts another log on the fire. It's so cold out there without her.

He bakes bread in the little old church, its wood graying with my hair, its roof sagging in the fading wheat of the field. And I reach out and Scott extends a cloud of bread to me—whole wheat, to purge me of myself.

tacoma, 3 a.m.

After a while, Freud stopped by. I heard him lurking in the bushes as I lay in bed and enticed images from the shadows. I imagined Freud stopping over and luring me out with a promise of one of his games. I imagined Darwin stepping from the bushes and both of them sucker punching, and eventually kicking the shit out of me, then digging in my pockets for spare change as I lie bleeding on the sidewalk, then walking off somewhere—they don't say where, but do mention in that flat, professional tone of theirs, as they are leaving, that I surely am not welcome.

Freud threw rocks at my window as I played with the moist shadows, pulling and stretching them. I knew he wanted to toss around a ball—he liked that. A quick game of horse, probably.

The rocks pissed me off, so I slipped into the bathroom and quickly returned with a freezing cold bucket of iodine which I dispatched onto his scraggly head.

I was content to trade baskets with him as I slipped into a fuzzy, hazy dream of you. I was an architect and you were my critic. "Your conscience: The twentieth century," I remember you calling yourself as I loped from side to side, like the lazy eye of a skinny, unpopular teenager with thick

tacoma, 3 a.m.

glasses and acne, as he's giving his 60-year-old science teacher who smells of mothballs the Heimlich, just for kicks. I scamper back down the court like the auto industry in cahoots with your barber as you recount to me that, in a letter, a five-year-old had scribbled in crayon on a napkin how the didactic idiom of the metaphor held the street edge, and therefore I did not understand the site, and, despite everyone's best efforts, probably never would.

It was as if I was standing in an open field as you whispered this to me with your sunny-day wind and the world began to end in horrors around me: taking elbows to the face; the inevitable polarization of my hair; halitosis in eighth grade gym class; the death of God; the proliferation of the insurance racket; tow trucks; an old man wheezing as he pushes his vegetable cart in Katmandu; an inner-city kid lighting a bundle of rags in the dark, dusty haze of a basement in a run-down tenement; a baby screaming and an indigent hacking a coal-mine disaster cough in an Embers in a lost, embarrassed suburb of our collective uncertainty; rural electrification; indoor plumbing; the internal combustion engine; the Merrimac listing slightly to the starboard; the opposable thumb; we leave the trees; we leave the ocean; cellular division; etc.

It sounded something like a lawn mower drowning in a vat of pea soup and whale blubber in the basement of a dirty little shoe factory outside Saigon circa 1932. It sounded like that, like one of those dirty little secrets. And it mattered to me in that way like when you forget to call and lose my number, even though you were the one who asked for it and I, being me, reluctantly gave it to you, as that was the only thing that I could do, I being me and all.

Just then my dad stepped out of the shadows. I hadn't seen him in months, although my parents' room was right

i'm right here

down the hall. I lived in the "web-footed only" part of the house, separated by customs, by what I referred to as "superstitions," a word my father wouldn't allow.

At one time, my father worked for the auto industry—on those secret projects to replace clean, efficient streetcars with noisy busses in cities all over the world. But that was a long time ago. For years now he has just watched daytime television, game shows mostly, in his easy chair up on the roof.

Superstitions, facts, "history"—clipped and pieced together, pasted haphazardly, randomly, lazily, in collages you call "life." Dirty little secrets. Dirty little basement secrets. Jazz stories. Jazz stories and dirty little secrets, boxed up in the basement, carefully written down and tabulated, all of them entitled "and." All of them encrypted with seven-digit numbers in volumes called "phone books" that some anonymous company mysteriously leaves at your door every year. From men in anonymous communist-brown work suits. Delivered in their anonymous communist-brown trucks. Left on crisp fall days. Left for you to wonder about.

I'm his dirty little secret. One of many, I suppose, littered throughout this reeking butt-town, scattered in the driveway—what they call "leaves"—misunderstanding the site, clouds passing by on the winds of old secrets, clouds swimming on fire, and leaves rustling, and the sky burbling. Those so-called delivery people are out there; although I refer to them as "archivists" in that language I have evolved over the years that I somehow courageously call "the truth."

He stepped out of the shadows. He had on a pair of my pajamas—the ones with little Richard Nixon faces all over them—and he opened me up with a haymaker to my breadbasket. One punch laid me out. He stood above me for a *tacoma, 3 a.m.*

moment, then he sauntered out from the driveway and wandered down the street with a prostitute who had once taught at my grammar school.

My insides imploded to squish down on themselves like an accordion in a cartoon. I tried to yelp, uncontrollably, but it only came out as a trolley squeaking to a stop in the snow and hitting an old Saigon man on a bike with a Saigon hat on who once killed a great king with his bare hands many years ago in a far off jungle on the other side of the world, but was now just the Saigon guy who lived down the street and stared into the school yard with calculating eyes, wondering secretively, proudly, about how he could influence this promising crop of young minds, and of all the changes he could sway in that surreptitious manner that only children seem to muster.

I collapsed. Cramps. I buckled up. Too much soup. Freud shook his head as he walked down the sidewalk to the dimly lit street in a haze of mist and lazily shook some change from my pocket in his wrinkled fist and hummed an obscure, unpopular Velvet Underground song and dreamt of his mother bathing on the shores of a muddy creek with two large sweaty men on a 98-degree day in Mississippi in 1936. I rolled around in a tight ball, clenching my gut. I watched as he put one of Eleanor Roosevelt's stockings over his sweaty, hopeful face, tucking it snugly as he worked it down his neck. I heard him kick-start the moped he stole. And I heard him putter off, with my favorite cans from my beer can collection connected with strands of my baby blanket clanging behind in a wonderful carbon dioxide haze as I clutched some hate mail I so resentfully forgot to send.

Too much pea soup maybe. Too much pizza maybe. I squeezed. My body tightened. Blisters of sweat bloomed. I felt like I was entangled in the greasy cables of an elevator shaft

i'm right here

with a wild boar in an anonymous auto industry high-rise.

It felt the way it feels when you don't call. It felt like when Dad walloped a haymaker to my breadbasket. It felt like Freud rolling drunks. It felt like the bus station in Reno at Christmas. It felt like the auto industry whispering to Darwin, who shakes his head and smiles slightly and winks back. It felt like an all-you-can-eat buffet at Pizza Hut—you don't get your money's worth unless you get that stinging cramp within two hours. It feels like I should have gone to Fat Lorenzo's (if you do, be sure to wear your winter boots—the rats bite).

Maybe we should've gone to some fancy place, to impress our friends, maybe gotten a bowl of cold noodles with a single, putrid slice of tomato on top—"spaghetti" I think they call it—all for twelve dollars. And we only had to wait an hour and a half for it.

Maybe we should have just had peanut butter and jelly sandwiches at my place, and then made out down in the boiler room. Either has its charms, but you didn't call, even though you assured me that you would, as you flogged an underpaid migrant worker as he picked your tomatoes and a baby giraffe gestated in my stomach and you gave birth to an elephant. I remember that day, such golden moments, shining now, ringing, rippling only in my memory, as if a pond, as if it never happened, as if I only dreamt it.

I waited all night

for you to call.

I crawled back to the house. I begged for a procedural review, but the phone company pretended not to hear. I crawled through the leaves.

Maybe I'll move back to Aberdeen . . . after all, tomorrow's another day.

tacoma, 3am

The sky spits and sputters and burbles like a baby on its back in a crib, and like the beautifully churning ocean as the Merrimac melts into the bubbles and begins to lilt into its beautiful sinking sleep. And I am beautiful. Clouds pass overhead and leaves rust and the ironclad spins slowly, frozen in its beautiful churning. And I know that, despite all of this, or, maybe because of it, I am still beautiful.

blue water, blue sky

part 1

It was my first day of work, or did I mention that? Anyway, as I was saying, I was in this large, empty apartment, just sitting there, about to begin my bit—which was, you know, easy to learn—or did I tell you that? Anyway, I'm welcomed in by this really skinny, short, pale guy in a suit that looked two or three sizes too big and as if it had never been in fashion. It was a weird shade of green, kind of a shiny olive. It looked very uncomfortable. I don't know, it was like "the lost suit" or something.

So this little guy leads me in. His body kind of tilts to the side. He looks very uncomfortable—I don't think it was the suit though. Anyway, as I said, I sit right down on the couch by the door. It was the only furnishing in the room other than a small photo of a butterfly up on the wall.

I open the little folder they gave me and pull out their brochure, when this large, dark man drags a smaller fellow into the room by his hair. This was an old place, very charming actually—the door and window framing were old and ornate, but painted over many times through the years. Anyway, this guy is dragged into the room, right before me.

His chest was ripped open and some important pieces of his insides were sort of hanging out. Blood soaked his coat and was flowing onto the hardwood floor.

I think he was dead but I'm not sure. He wasn't really breathing, and he didn't really moan at all. He was just lying there. All I could do was play it cool, just couch there to let 'em know I was hep to whatever jive was going down.

The big guy reached down into this guy's gut and pulled some stuff out. You know, innards. Right in front of me. He pulled up a handful, showed them to the little guy in the lost suit, then turned and threw them at the corner. I don't know if he was trying to hit a wall or the corner, but those innards didn't get far. They were really heavy, you could tell. They just slapped the wood floor like a wet mop.

The big guy went over to them and began stomping on them. I mean he had these good dress shoes on. The little guy next to me just nodded and nodded and sort of looked on and said, "His spleen," as if he were commenting to me and yet just talking to himself.

The big guy paid a lot of attention to this spleen. He was concentrating intently on it, obviously very upset with it as he muttered obscenities and slipped around, trying to catch himself against the wall as he pressed it into the floor with all his weight.

The room was white; I remember that very well. It was an old, fuzzy white—very hazy. The kind of hazy room where shadows just fade right into the cloudy walls.

Anyway, the little guy stared across the room for a moment as the big guy worked on the spleen, slipping around and cussing under his breath, then he took a step forward and looked straight down at the guy. He bent down and stared right into him. The guy on the floor sort of coughed a sputter. Then another.

i'm right here

Now I don't even know if a guy needs his spleen, but I quickly slipped the brochure back in the folder, stood, and slid out the door. I walked down the hall very fast, my shadows bouncing in front of me, three of them swaying back and forth under the weak, faded light. These shadows bounced on the floor and the walls and the ceiling, stretching out miles in front of me, each reaching for other times. But it was like they weren't my shadows. They were strangers, as if connected to someone else.

Yeah, that hall was the same hazy white as the room. Like a hazy day outside when the sky is that old, deep, faded-white color—you know how the sky gets.

I remember wondering if I should call the ambulance or the cops. And I wondered if those guys were mobsters, or loan sharks, or gamblers, or dealers, or if they were from the government, and as I ran down the hall, those shadows bouncing in front of me, I wondered if a guy really needs his spleen. I mean, could a guy really get on without his spleen?

Anyway, as I was saying, I went straight back and quit. It was my first day, so naturally they followed me out, trying to convince me that it was only my first shot at it and I should expect rejections and that I should stay on and all. But I never did get around to finding out if a guy really needed his spleen or not.

The next day, I got another job with this other place, you know, the same type of outfit. Funny thing, I was sent to the same block, a brick apartment right across from the one the day before. I knocked on the first door; a lady in her sixties answered and I did their little intro bit to get inside. She invited me in and I sat down on the couch.

There was all this garbage all over the place. I mean all over. Everywhere. All kinds of garbage. The room had older furniture in it, but it was nice. I mean it was OK. And here all this garbage was there—tons of it—all around, everywhere. I mean it was tucked under the couch and chairs and behind stuff and under dishes and stuffed in lamp shades and stuffed under the cushions. Listen to me now, I mean it was all around, yet kind of hidden in a sad, obvious way.

This lady waded through a bit of garbage and sat down on a chair. She faced me and I slowly opened their folder and pulled out their brochure. But, it was like I was doing it all real slowly, like I couldn't believe this place. There was this lady just sitting there smiling at me with all this garbage piled, pitifully hidden away, and this old guy shuffled into the room and right past me and shuffled into another room on this rug that was crinkling and bulging with garbage underneath it. I just couldn't believe how people could live with all that garbage around them like that.

part II

I ran into this girl on the street the next day. I had seen her around and thought quite highly of her—her textured voice, the willowy way she swayed, her bright clothes, her wide smile, her billowing long blond hair. "Hey, how are you," she said when we met, but that was just like her to say something like that, wasn't it.

I mumbled to her shyly and we exchanged pleasantries and as we parted I watched over my shoulder as she slid away. I couldn't tell you how many times I've watched girls slide away from me like that.

I was embarrassed somehow, ashamed that I couldn't talk to her, couldn't hold her there longer, couldn't come up with anything more clever or interesting to say. I was ashamed that I didn't have anything to say to girls like that, that I was too quiet, or embarrassed that I wasn't anything more than what I was. I was ashamed that I didn't have anything more to offer than a polite hello.

I always seem to hope for more than those polite hellos, but in this town if you don't play in a band, you're pretty much invisible to girls. Or maybe it was just me. Maybe it was me who was invisible. I had no identity after all, nothing to offer, nothing to speak of, nothing to hang my hat on.

I was looking up into the sky as I walked. I was searching into that vibrant blue, staring into that blue water, wading through that blue sky, hoping to find myself in there, hoping to find something, some lucky life to crawl into.

Everyone always asks me how things are going, but no one wants to hear the truth. All they want to hear about is how good things are. Well, they aren't so good right now. Maybe I expect too much. Or maybe I just feel too much. No one wants to hear about such things though. People just nod politely, thinking that something's wrong with you if you talk about things like that. It makes them uncomfortable. They think you're weak if things aren't TV-show perfect. People only want to hang out with winners, after all.

I had been living in an abandoned railroad caboose. A faded sky blue. Down by the river. Mud was everywhere. The river was thick with brown water. The trees of the river bank hung over my shack. It was as if I lived in a cave. And large rocks dotted the area, so you had to crouch and balance from one rock to another in order to get to my place.

One day I showed up after work and the caboose was gone. Vanished. It was all gone, all my stuff. Just like that. Life is like that though.

Those kinds of things didn't bother me anymore. They used to. In fact, I'd wasted entire days thinking about such things. But I had become used to them. Next, I filled my days with finding a place for myself in this life. I'm not sure exactly what that could be, but God, it must be out there somewhere.

I thought about that girl a lot too. I dreamt of wading into the blue water of her eyes. I thought about getting lost in the blue sky of her life. I pondered wrapping her life around me. I felt her sneaking into my blue water. I felt her tiptoeing off with my blue sky.

Maybe I'll move out to the country, out to the blue water, out to the blue sky, out to a narrow creek where I could feel the clouds move through me, where I could feel the cool water run through me, where I could feel the sky. I long to feel those things, to feel a part of something real.

It feels like there's something missing from my life. I don't know what that could be. A good job. Friends. A nice place to live. A girlfriend. A cool car. Something clever or impressive to brag about. I don't know. It just feels like a mirage up ahead... I need it... yet I can't quite make it out. I feel it stirring out there, but I don't know what it could be.

part III

The next day they sent me to this little old house down the road from a hennery, across from a retirement home, and next to an auto salvage yard. The auto yard had a high, rusty corrugated fence encircling it protectively. Old auto parts were on display, leaning against the fence. And all day long the old folks had to sit and look out on all those parts, just sitting there, right in front of them.

i'm right here

I wore my lucky tie (for good luck, you know) the one I got at the secondhand shop just down the dirt road—a gold tie with faded bloodstains and bullet holes. Mass-murder chic is in, you know.

I rapped on the door and an old guy let me in. He led me into a square grandma-type living room—hothouse warm, pastel and lacy. He mumbled to himself as he peeked secretively across the street through the closed curtains of the large picture window that looked out at the neighborhood like a great omniscient eye. He spoke through a tight, disorganized face, with a smile you could light a match on—a composition not at all reassuring.

I tried, but I couldn't get a word in.

"I'll tell ya, what I saw last night sickened me. . ." he began in a broken voice that whined of a freight train slowing, uncooperative with hidden momentum—a potato famine of a voice. "Painting those paintings on his garage door—Adam and Eve shedding their ape-like fur, as images of skies and clouds and rivers and trees churn and twist to become one. What did he call it? 'In the garden of Eden: From Monkey to Man—It All Happened in One Afternoon.' And that siding of his, that jazzy collage—stainless steel, sheet metal, glass block, I-beams, cinder block—symbolizing the mongrelization of society, in direct action against the Aryan purity of our Mies van der Rohe modernist glass villa. I have nothing to hide! Do I look like someone with something to hide?!!"

I sat there shrugging attentively, holding out the brochure like a child with a bad report card.

"Hell's bells. You ask me, that boy's loony—just plain shit-eating delirious," he pointed over to me. His arm was shaking. "In the good ol' days we'd just drag freaks like that into the fields for a good ol' country whuppin'. No questions asked. Straighten 'em right up. Hell, if this was 300 years ago we'd be burnin' some poor left-handed sap at the stake right now. An' I know who'd be lightin' that first match . . . what's he doin' now, Isidore? Oh my, he's up on the roof again, gyratin' his pelvis like some sicko . . . what's that? Mother of creation, looks like he's prancin' around with the Old Testament above his head again," he coughed a couple of times and covered his mouth politely with the back of his sleeve. " Isidore, . . . oh, God . . . get my thirty-thirty."

His breath filled my face with a musty attic smell. His sentences dripped, his words flicked, his dry reasoning cracked with the sound of a leaking roof.

I slipped out the door and snuck down the narrow sidewalk between his house and the neighbor's. The houses around here are all so close. Everyone's packed in so tight. Tight little houses and tight little lives.

As I passed the front, out of the corner of my eye, I noticed him standing in the picture window of the living room. He was banging on the window. Bang bang bang. With both fists raised in the darkness. "You're a butterfly! You're a butterfly!" he insisted over and over in a tight, muffled yell of a cough. "You're a butterfly, goddamn you!" Then he tapped on the great window with a crowbar.

I waved politely and began to run. I put my hands in my pockets, as the wind was picking up. And it was then that I realized that as I ducked out, I had accidentally snatched a small clock off the end table in his living room. I don't know why—I was just tryin' to get outta there; it just ended up in my hand as I tooled around the corner.

I worked it in my hands as I walked. It was very ornate—old and gold plated, with an old ornate butterfly encased inside of it.

I ended up trying another grandma house just like the previous one. A skinny, robotic little fellow led me in and

i'm right here

offered a couch. He staked his claim to an easy chair opposite me. "Yep yep, yer one a dem chaps, ain't ya," he squeaked. "Lessee, I got me one a dem hair replacements last year—but not on my noodle—no no, all over my body. Got more hair now than three fellers half my age could boast—drives the chickies mad, don't ya know." He winked and clucked, then cleared his throat and reached up to remove his prosthetic head. He lowered it carefully to set it to rest on his lap. Then recognizing his faux pas, in embarrassment, he clumsily lifted it from his lap and leaned over to set it on the coffee table between us, careful to position it to face the wall away from me. He fumbled with it and his head slipped away, rolling off the table onto the floor between his legs. "Oh that's OK," he picked it off the floor, dusting it off with his palm. "I got me several others. They're up on a shelf in the other room." A small, mechanical echo growled from his flat neck. "Yep, got me this one a few months back—a real beaut." The voice wisped moistly from the shiny medical plastic and cheap prosthetic steel cap, or stump, that was his neck. "People call me Stump—Stump or Stumpy," he nodded.

We exchanged pleasantries and gradually Stumpy began faintly uttering a foreign tongue:

"*C2=2e / Fy (Fa + 12e2/ 23 (k2)2*   *2rt=24-25*
C=[1/2 (kd) (b)} (Fc) = 1/2 kfCbd   i / c = bd2 / 6
bd3-12A / Gb (d2-b2)2   70 X (6.1)2 / 8 = 325.6 kN-n
32d / 4a = M 4.8 x (20)2 / 240 kip-fit   M / Fb = I / c = A (Wd2 / 4)
t = d / 4 = (w) d4 / 32 = c (d / 2)   *Fc = [l—1/3 [(Lid)4 / k] 2]?*"

he inquired softly.

blue water, blue sky

```
                    "north  S 6 5 3
west  S A 9 8              H Q J 9      east  S 10 2
      H A K 7 6 4          D A K J 9          H 10 8 2
      D 10 5 4             C A J 5            D 8 7 2
      C 8 3 2                                 C 10 9 6 3 2
                    south  S K Q J 7 4
                           H 5 3
                           D 6 3
                           C K Q 4"
```

I offered politely.

"Sub rosa tempus fugit, vade mecum mirabile dictu! Inter nos,"

he replied.

"Yes, yes, time flies secretly—it goes with me. Marvelous to relate! It remains just between us, that is,"

I spat.

"Difference in recall of B = PI	$y = 429 [1-e (CA / 6.675)]$
$rxy = E (xy) / NoXoYp + q = 1.00$	$Br = (R\text{-}S) / (A\text{-}S)$
0-20	idiot	$p = 6$ X Sum of d2 / N (N2—1) rAA =
		$AR1i / 1 + (A\text{-}1) r1i$
20-50	imbecile	$V = 100(O) / M$ (tri) R / R = K
		$z = X—M / SD$
50-70	moron	$Qp = p + a$ (1—p)—bp IQ = MA / CA X
		100 Exy / N
70-90	*dull normal*	$h = 1 / (sgr)2 X M$ *EQ = EA/CA X 100*
		$k = (sqr) 1—rr2,$"

he reported matter-of-factly.

"1 can cream of mushroom soup
1 can tuna

i'm right here

1 box ring or shell noodles (7 oz.)
1/2 can peas
1. Boil noodles, drain. 2. Mix ingredients in 2-qt. casserole dish. Crumble potato chips on top. 3. Heat in oven at 350 degrees for 30 minutes,"

I reasoned.

"Game 6:

Cincinnati	AB	H	R	RBI	New York	AB	H	R	RBI
Rose, 3b	5	1	2	0	Rivers, cf	4	0	2	0
Griffey, rf	4	0	1	0	White, lf	3	0	0	0
Morgan, 2b	4	1	1	1	Munson, c	5	0	3	0
Perez, 1b	4	0	0	0	Chambliss, 1b	5	1	1	0
Driessen, dh	3	2	3	1	May, dh	4	0	0	0
Foster, lf	4	1	2	2	Nettles, 3b	2	0	0	0
Bench, c	4	0	2	0	Gamble, rf	3	0	1	1
Geronimo, cf	4	1	1	1	Piniella, rf	1	0	0	0
Concepcion, ss	4	0	1	1	Randolph, 2b	4	0	0	0
Zachry, p	0	0	0	0	Stanley, ss	1	0	0	0
McEnaney, p	0	0	0	0	Mason, ss	1	1	1	1
					Ellis, p	0	0	0	0
					Tidrow, p	0	0	0	0
totals	36	6	13	6		35	2	8	2,"

he sighed.

"$Ba[NO_3]2$ $(Ch_3)2$ $(C_6H_6)2$ $BaCO_3$ naphthalene L-dopa,"

I retorted with a grin.

"To be sure,"

he smiled.

blue water, blue sky

I leaned back and sighed. I felt I was finally getting good at this, this give and take—at last, I was finally getting good at something, finally feeling good about something, finally getting a chance to do something, to be something.

Through the window I noticed the bronze dome of the basilica, searching comfortingly above the lazy trees and timid roofs in the hazy distance.

The man lifted himself robotically and motioned me into the little kitchen. I rose and followed him into the small formica room, through a thin door, and down into the basement. On the door hung a rotting trout tied to a rusty nail by a fraying string. It clung to the sadness of the peeling white door—a nice avant-garde touch, if you ask me. A polite gesture. For my benefit, no doubt.

Suddenly imbued with a manic energy, he bounced down the narrow wooden stair and shuffled me past some of his compositions taped on the wall next to the washtub. Photos of butterflies clipped from an old encyclopedia hung next to them. I glanced at the titles as we passed: "The Night Begins to Moan," "A Stranger in the Mirror," "A Beautifully Phonic Personage, So Far Away, So Far Away—You Will Forget Me." Titles so dangerous they stung.

He had rows and rows of tall, straight, gray filing cabinets and an old copying machine. "I Xerox a lot," he said. "I run a tight ship around here." The basement was stark and clean—just bare concrete floor and walls, just waiting.

"Ever been attacked by a pack of wild dogs?" he panted mistily, as if he could snap his fingers dryly and I'd be frantically stumbling down an alley, limbs flapping sloppily, with a half-dozen assorted dogs in hot pursuit.

I gazed rhetorically at the card tables before me. "Everyday."

i'm right here

"Well then you'll be good and safe down here, my friend."

I intuited something about him. I wondered if I should leave, or if I should ask to move in and stay awhile.

He gestured to the card tables before us. They were filled with tools and wires and what looked to be several old tube-style vacuum cleaners hooked together. They hummed a faint whisper. "Is that a ham radio?"

"Well, hee-hee, sort of," he stepped up to tinker with some of the electrical junk scattered on the card tables. "I built my own toaster," he pointed. "My own radio," he nodded. "My own vacuum, and this, my own double-tubed occulus of the vesticator," he bent over and fiddled with some switches. "I don't know, maybe I popped a head bolt," he shrugged. "Maybe blew out another head pipe. Maybe I smoked another mind compressor," he shook his shoulders as if his head were still attached. "I'll try to tune someone in," he said in a smoky exhale. And sure enough, a faint, distant chirping began to smooth out into a hazy whisper. He held up a finger as if listening, as he adjusted a little dial.

"Mafoi! Magni nominis umbra Malisavibus Mauvaise honte Mauvais quart d'heure Mirabile visu monde Monumentum aere perennius Mutato nomine de te fabula narratur!"

"See," he chuckled. "It works. I can hear what they're thinking." He turned and looked up to me. "I can hear them thinking."

"Mafoi! Magni nominis umbra Malisavibus Mauvaise honte Mauvais quart d'heure Mirabile visu monde Monumentum aere perennius Mutato nomine de te fabula narratur!"

"That decoded loosely translates to . . . hold on . . . It's coming through . . . It loosely translates to: 'My faith! Indeed! In the shadow of a great name. Under evil auspices. Bad shame. Bad quarter hour (an uncomfortable, though brief, experience). Wonderful to behold. Beautiful world. A moment more lasting than bronze.' And finally, 'With the name changed, the story applies to you,'" he nodded and nodded. "I can hear them thinking. I can hear them. . . . I'll try to tune into someone else now. That nut-job Lempkin down the block. That fetal regression therapist. Let's see what he's up to. Let's see what he's thinking . . ."

At that, I stepped back quietly. I stepped back to the wall and turned to pull myself up. I wiggled through one of the narrow basement windows. Once outside I stood and brushed myself off. I walked around the tidy little house to wander back up the sidewalk. As I walked I pulled the little list of names and addresses from the pocket of my plaid jacket, checking it carefully: Dooley Womack, Eddie Stanky, Al McBean, Russ McCool. I crumpled it and tossed it aside. It skidded into the gutter and rolled under some tired leaves. Screw them.

Walking back home I ran into that little birdie again. A heat can flew overhead and that really heavy cream stepped up. She was a saucy dish, really into the oil, a real heat artist—with some seriously heavy sugar, some serious iron. I heard she was on the heavy, but you never know about things you hear—maybe, maybe not, you know. "Man, that jump band had a great load of hay, the leaping jeebies, a Milwaukee goiter, a nice little piece of furniture, giving me the wearies," she was lightin' some heesh, offered some as she passed, but this herman stepped up so she had to butterfly.

She made me nervous. Nervous and embarrassed, I'm not proud to report. And I'm not exactly sure why. It might've been a lot of things—that I didn't have a cool job. That I didn't have a lot of friends, like all those people on TV. That they always seem to ask *how it's going, how's work?* and look at you, at your clothes and your shoes and your hair, as if those things have anything to do with anything. It was a lot of things like that.

I mumbled to her shyly as I looked over my shoulder and watched her drift away. I was embarrassed and ashamed that I couldn't talk to her, couldn't come up with anything clever or more interesting. I know most guys think they're so great, so great that if they puked all over a girl they'd consider it a compliment, a present even. But I was ashamed that I wasn't something more interesting, something more.

I heard her footsteps on the sidewalk behind me. They seemed so full, and sounded like she was walking away with something of mine.

I stood at a stoplight, waiting for everything to pass. I noticed my reflection in the mud puddle below my feet in the gutter, the clouds floating by. I felt ashamed to look at myself—I was twenty-three, and nothing good had ever happened to me.

part IV

As for me, well, I guess I'm still trying to find myself, hoping someone will let me, hoping I'll get a chance. I haven't seen that girl around in a while. I stopped going out, moved into a fort I made for myself inside the trestle of an old oar dock—a giant rhythmic centipede of sleeping history. The trains clickity-clack in the distance. The oar starts here and ends up in our driveways. And we miss the entire process. And I tool around in my vespa scooter at an insane velocity, crazily tempting centrifugal force and the presumed laws of physics, satisfying my need to be connected to the outside world—for a time I could only handle it at that blur level, hiding in it, denying reality yet again.

Just to let you know, I finally settled in as a bus driver— steering the city—preferring to just sit there and allow the world to flow around me, a place where I can feel a little safer, a place where I can search for my place, for a contentment, for something to be.

I put that butterfly clock up on the dashboard of the bus. A nice homey touch. And the people compliment me on it. The regulars are pretty nice that way—and it took a while, but I guess I'm happy to drive them around, and to be a part of their lives.

hated

In the past, people seemed to dislike me because I was considered successful, which is to say I had a job. Then, after things went bad at the company, I was viewed with hostility because I didn't have a job and was considered a bum. I've been despised for other arbitrary reasons as well, of course—for being too loud or too quiet at a party, for example. I've been misunderstood for the socks that I wear, or for the ones that I don't. I've been loathed for the ideas that I have. I've been viewed with horror for the schools that I've attended. I've fallen into disfavor for the toothpaste I use. I've been alienated for the direction in which my hair has been combed. And, of course, I've been ignored for the way in which I park my car.

I wake up in the morning and they start in on me—insecure hate mongers, jealous resentful paranoids, schmoozing phonies, brown-nosing asskissers, bossy control freaks, lazy crybabies—and I never really figured out why.

I don't have any friends to speak of anymore. They've all moved away or have gotten themselves married. And the people at work haven't really taken to me either. Which means I must be an easy target. No one gets ganged up on when they have friends around.

hated

Over the years I've slowly been pushed out to the edge of town. Not the "New" edge of town, with its sharp green lawns and muffler shops. Mine is the edge of town that no one talks about. The edge you tiptoe on. The edge with the unpaved roads, mud puddles, doors hanging crooked on their hinges, weeds growing tall in the hard ground, paint peeling like leaves, porches leaning in a frozen wait, the sky an open yawn. Where the local cowpunchers dump the bodies. Where time hangs heavy. There is no place left to go but here. This is the end of it all.

Since I moved out here it's been a steady routine of work and TV. And it must've just gotten too bloody much to bear, watching me and the house slowly fading away. That moping trance nipping at me in tight tugs of jobs and promises—coming and going and groceries and bus stops and laundry and all that other life stuff coming and going, flashing on and off, life smoothing me off at the corners. So much so that even the trees out here hold me in bitter contempt. You'd think they'd recognize one of their own. You'd think they'd show the slightest bit of courtesy at least. You'd think they'd put in a good word for me. But they seem to be lost in their own treeness. Or maybe it's just me, maybe I expect too much from the trees.

As for everything else . . . I seem to be an irritant to the telephone poles. The road turns its back on me. The tableware has a grudge against me, as do the lamps, photographs, farming implements, sock drawers, encyclopedias— oh, how I could go on about encyclopedias . . .

I started off with an impressive set—full, fresh, clean, and innocent. The tallest man you've ever seen sold them to me. Tall as hell. I think he was a Mormon. A young guy. A skinny bastard. Frizzy mothball hair. Pencil thin and seven feet if he was an inch. I remember him well. Long pallid face. Intense beady gerbil eyes. Bony fingers like whips. Was one scary son of a bitch.

It was the hottest day you could think of, too. That skinny bastard was all rusty, cold, and stiff. "All that they taught you, all you need to know . . ." he'd say, tapping that string of a finger on a sample volume." Every family needs one . . . you want to provide the best for your family . . . it's the American way . . . it's the American dream . . . a dream of dreams and a dream of dreamers . . ."

Through the years that set sort of took a beating. They're all in fine shape mostly, but volumes come and go you know, with children moving out and moving back and wives leaving and coming back and friends and relatives and neighbors coming and going and moving all over and then back and forth again to the dullest houses and apartments ever. To very unencyclopedic places.

I got other ones. Replacements. New ones and old ones. From garage sales and library sales and church bazaars and secondhand shops; not the originals, but I did the best I could. It's still a full set, though a rather jumbled one. At one time or another there were several volumes of "H," maybe half a dozen "Gs," all from different sets. I had the World Book, Britannica, and all the rest, a shelf full of colors and sizes.

It was about this point that I put up that sign in the lawn to keep people like that tall son of a bitch away. It was one of those futile gestures that I thought would somehow keep that damn set together once and for all.

It just got to be too much though, all that coming and going, the distrust of my hair, the rejection of my furniture, the haunting of my garbage, the horror of where my TV was positioned, the irritation of my socks, the spite of my tooth-

hated

paste, the hostility of my mailbox, the revulsion of how I parked my car. I just gave up trying. I had been in it all too long and it had all just run right through me and after a while the house and all really began to show it and my hate just got up one day and abandoned it all. Who could blame it.

I remember it was unusually early. I woke one morning, alone as usual in my 6-by-4 coffin of a bedroom. I woke and all the hate was gone. Just like that. I sat on the edge of my bed, fresh from the warm water of sleep, drying off as the sun rose, the room stirring from its blackness, focusing from a dark indigo into a tight purple.

There it was in the corner, just sitting there. It was big and thick and ripe. It was baggy and heavyset.

"I'm leaving you," my hate said from the corner.

"OK," I said rubbing my eyes, politely acknowledging the statement. (I had been very used to the routine) "How are you going this time?" I asked politely in that friendly chitchat of mine. I had seen it leave by almost every means imaginable; burning down the garage, flooding the basement, poisoning the doughnuts, college, transfer, illness, eight-story window, note scribbled on a T-shirt or spray painted on the living room wall. Carol took my lamp, Betty packed up my faith in the postal service, Maggie plundered my thoughts on Mayan ruins, Sissy snuck off with my smile, Jeannie ransacked my silverware, Judy abducted my optimism, Samantha plagiarized my emotions, Diane looted my dreams . . . and I began getting smaller and smaller and smaller . . . a little more empty, a little more distant.

"I need to find myself," it said after a moment, its voice smooth as a summer wind. "I just can't take this anymore," it finally admitted to the morning.

"Of course," I shrugged, excusing it. "Well, you know where the door is." I rubbed my eyes more in the soothing light. I stood and moved to the window. Everything was bright and clean, and I saw it walk on down the walk. I didn't even hear the door open. It carried an encyclopedia under its arm.

After a quiet moment my son Beeno shuffled in. He was wearing a bright orange T-shirt and a ransom note of a smile. His shirt yawned in bright yellow letters:

I AM NOT
YOUR ENEMY

"How was church?" I rubbed my eyes.

"I don't know. . ." He shrugged " I couldn't stop laughing." He chewed his gum slowly, making sucking sounds like a cow walking in mud.

His earphones blared a song by his band, "The McNuggin Fluffers." It was their hit single "Laundry Room," a composition of him and his delinquent buddies beating the washing machine in the basement with baseball bats and tire chains.

He bobbed his head to the dirge, holding up a finger. "Yeah, this part—that sharp pinging . . . right there . . . that was Nigel on the crowbar," he said smacking his gum. "Hope ya had a good old-fashioned bad dream." He turned and walked out the door, still bobbing his head. "I'm gonna go jam out in the garage. I got me a hankerin' ta wail. Got me a few more songs in me ta work out. One's called 'Lawn Mower,' I think. Trevor's comin' over with his chalkboard. We're startin' up a chalkboard band."

His previous band, "Monkey Smells Good," played moody songs about sexual relations with primates, material

hated

which was ultimately deemed too narrow artistically, so they disbanded after only a few short, tragic days.

My other son, Bunny, was perched in his chair at the end of the hall, staring at a blank wall as usual, a favorite activity of his. His girlfriend Boom-Boom sketched fatal automobile accidents at his feet.

A few days later I was just a smooth erosion of past possibilities. All that hate dropped by for a visit. I was up on the roof having a cigarette. I think it was in town on some business. It had gained a little more weight in the middle there, and looked a bit flush, but mostly it looked the way I remember. I recall hearing it had gotten into sales, door to door stuff. Encyclopedias, I think, but I'm not sure if it stuck with it or not.

"Nice of you to drop by," I said searching for the rising sun. Shadows grew longer and the bare yard turned colors—dark purples and greens, like a bruise.

"I was in the neighborhood," it said. I climbed down and we sat on the cold concrete steps. The sun simmered through the deep shadows of the trees in the distance, emerging a deep orange, flickering behind the fence of old trees that balanced on the horizon, pushing the refinery into the distance, into its own respective corner.

"You're looking like a smooth erosion of past possibilities," it coughed.

"I thought so," I said gazing out at the trees gathering before us.

The wind was blowing the leaves off the roof and down upon us like a slow, gentle rain. The gusts of giant rain took the last few strands of hair from the top of my head and some shingles off the roof and spun them down into the little valley of rolling weeds and mud below.

"I finally got a sex drive when I was thirty-seven. Damnedest distraction ever." I shook my head. "Lucky for me it only lasted three weeks."

"Everything leaves," it wheezed, covering its mouth with the back of its palm.

"Why?"

"Evolution, I suppose. Go with the flow," it nodded. "And appreciate things while you can."

"I'll try," I whispered.

"I'll tell you one thing though, I met myself today. Yep. What I saw sickened me to no end. And there was no relief from it," he sighed, his eyes narrowing. "I was walking down the street and there I noticed myself standing up ahead of me on the corner up ahead. I stopped and watched myself step up into a bus, and as the bus passed I saw myself looking out at me from the bus, and the me inside the bus gave me a really dirty look, like it was really mad at me."

Then Beeno burst out the door and jumped over us. He cleared the steps and hit the hard ground running. He flailed his arms wildly and shrieked, "It's a maaaaaadhouse!" at the top of his lungs, like he did every morning on the way to the bus stop that waited up the gravel road.

We didn't say anything.

The bells of the church pealed in the distance.

I watched those trees for awhile, then my old hate had to leave. For some reason I half expected it to mutter some sappy drivel about "tolerance" or "kindness," or some such gibberish, but it didn't. It just mumbled something about how the truth was "an elusive and rare commodity" and about how everyone was trying to sell you something, to try to make themselves look better. "My advice to you . . ." it slowly nodded, "is to try to find the good in everyone." Then it got up and left me sitting on the steps thinking.

hated

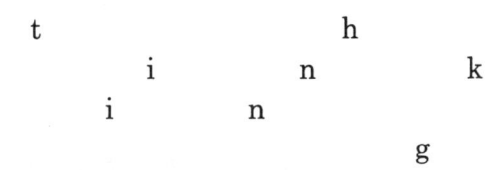

    t   h
       i   n   k
i   n
                g

    "You're a good old hate," I finally said to it as it puttered off in its rusted out pickup. It bobbed slowly across the grassy waves and followed that necklace of trees out of sight. Its license plate said "forgive."
    The sun began to rise, to pull me into the day, to heal me into the night. To heal me into the setting sun. To push me into some unforeseen kindness, some unforeseen comfort.
    I held my breath, closed my eyes, reached out, held those shadows in my hands. And the clouds rolled in like waves.

bird in flight

1. The boy walks along the side of the road. The little old school bus lurches ahead. The bus is old—small yellow short curvaceous freckled with rust and dust—engine cussing sputtering seats rattling windows shaking on the soft sandy road. The road grows like a nervous vine—slithering and rolling over the subtle hills and around and through and between the golden wheat field's gentle undulations and windblown desires.

The wind blows designs and messages, struggling to communicate. The wind doubles back to chase itself. It is young and exuberant. It whips around the boy and somersaults across the road and through the tilted gray fence posts and rolls back into the field.

The kid's jacket is old, unimaginably old, inconceivably plaid, and fantastically faded. Old and faded and sublimely plaid, draining red and thirsty black, receding further into the past with each day, with each gentle breath.

2. The boy sits alone in the middle of the small yellow curves. He tucks his pale head down as the bright sun burrows in. It wipes his face. It brushes his cheeks. It rubs his short, endlessly black hair. With the magical rattling incan-

bird in flight

tation of windows, the sandy tan rug rolls out to bow before his feet. The boy has a long walk ahead.

    3. The road is a cloudy sigh—old and tired, creaking and shy. The empty mirror of sky is clear with a soft blue—transparent, unfocused, lazy, wandering. The calm wind separates the two, like an ocean.

    4. This time it is winter. The road is hard and clear. The fields are covered in a lifetime of white, buried under a four-foot tomorrow of snow. The naked sun glances off the jacket as it rushes along. The wind rolls past in heavy gusts, looking and looking, like a dog off a leash—this way and that—for something to push and roll.

    I see this kid get off an old creaking bus. He skips along an old creaking road. His head is down. The sun is a sharp, bare bulb clinging to some distant ceiling. And at that moment, as the bus starts back up the slight hill, pushing itself slowly, a bird floats overhead in an empty blue freshness. And it is this moment exactly, I remember it all so well—it is at this moment that I want to tell you about it, it all seems so damn urgent. It all appears so monumental, so important somehow. It's at this moment exactly that I want to tell you something.

    5. A black bird soars across the sky as the boy walks. All is quiet and still but for the wind rolling in the golden wheat. The bird drifts away.

    6. I do not know him. I've never seen him before. But seeing him here, trudging along, I feel a certain warmth somehow, a certain love for him and this place. I do, I think—I think I do love him in that brotherly way. I think dearly of

i'm right here

him—alone in this place, in its spontaneous distilled essence—in its grounded solitude and perseverance, in its beautiful contradictions. I speak kindly of him. I seem to love him, don't I? I seem to love him like a God—and thus I feel that I am, somehow, becoming God.

    7. And now it's summer again. It's hot, the field's grass is thick and blowing, tall green and yellow flowing. A. Road. B. Bus. C. Boy. D. Wheat. E. Bird. F. Sky. G. Sun. H. Dry. And now I feel that I could be the bird, looking down on the steamy field, with its invisible heat rising, all flat and blank, and its crooked rough road like a wrinkle on its face—but a thin groove—the bus a tired beetle. Road. Bus. Boy. Wheat. Bird. Sky. Sun. Dry. It all rolls by so fast.

    8. And now I feel that I might be the bus. A slight inclination, an interest, a possibility. I might be the bus. I will not object to this. We are who we are after all. I will not object to this—to trying this on for a while.

    He is inside of me now. I can feel him stirring in the sun, sitting there alone—so quiet, so small.

    His name is Dell. So simple. Dell O'Dell. I bet you think that's a peculiar name, an amusement. I bet you think it's a real hoot—a real gasser. I bet your name would cause me to all but shit and piss myself.

    9. And now I'm the summer. Here I am. By all accounts it looks and feels like I'm the summer, like I'm growing—elusive and undefined; like I'm reaching, stirring, stretching. Hot, dry, brittle.

    I'm bigger now—an entire season. I think it's better to be an entire season, an entire time—full of moments. How lucky I must be.

bird in flight

Is it better to be so full, so anchored—growing, rippling out—or is it better to be but a bird in flight? One dot? A speck of dust? To be floating, to soar free?

```
10.      Sky                  Fence
    Road         Bus           Bird
         Boy          Wheat         Wind
              Bird          Sky
         Sun      (Take your pick)
```

11. My temper becomes the summer, my belief in the future like the bird. Would you want to end up as the old bus? Bald tires black knobs rock stupid hard seats hot rattling crunching gravel and stale air and dust and dust. And now I feel, watching all of this, that I might be the bus again. Not my turn. An epiphany, an involuntary guest appearance, a substitution, I think. And it's damn cold out. Pale yellow skin raw scratchy baked oil. Why do I always have to be the damn bus?

12. Now I'm the boy's jacket. Then I'm the sky—so warm, what a wonderful feeling—a flat, one-dimensional shiftless brother to the fields. A nervous conversation. A desperate hope. An unanswered prayer. A lost dream—a companion, mirror, poor cousin, lost twin, brooding temptress, genetic defect, nervous tic, two quarts of milk and some butter, neighbor girl's bra hanging on the clothesline, old friend found face down in the obituaries on a Saturday morning.

And who am I now? Would you tell me? I'm betting against it. I want to be the summer again. Could I? Am I the hero yet? Or am I the goat? Am I the terrible monster? Am I

i'm right here

the smug mirror? Or just an innocent dupe? Am I Hitler's monocle again? Am I Hitler's mustache yet? Am I Halderman's mug?

Am I a part of it all again, or just another cowering, obscure wet turd in someone else's sweaty, unfashionably plaid polyester trousers? Am I Dink Hawthorn, surfer in a '60s B movie? Am I "story as machine?" Does the #12 begin to fold and rotate over the #9? With steel girders to hold it in place? Does the #5 begin to extend and telescope hydraulically? Is the #3 rattling, in need of some adjustment or maintenance? Am I the hero yet? Will I get the girl soon?

The sun could be named Glen. The bus, Buddy. The field, Bubba. The road, Earl. The jacket, Sylvia. What is a bus? What is the summer? What is a jacket? When can I be any one of these? When can I be the cowboy? When can I be the zookeeper? When can I get the girl? When can I love someone I've never met before? When can I be Godlike? When can I be a "nice guy?"

13. The kid becomes a small bedroom on the second floor, his nose a deceptively simple old wooden nightstand, alone in the room, its drawer slightly ajar. His eyes are the white curtains fluttering in the half-open windows on either side of the nightstand. Light shines in as jagged shadows tattoo the hazy fuzz of wall, oscillating in and out of focus, beginning to evaporate into a vast stare of sky.

14. It's years later, or moments, perhaps. Tricks of incessant perception abruptly grow and argue like a prearranged marriage between the tired bus and burning wind. Power lines rot on gray wooden poles, like a lost America lying in wait.

bird in flight

I saw the jacket as a sort of mythical "Lost America", the bus as a personal Mayflower; the field a Columbus; the power lines an interloper, an unwanted guest; the passage of time an observer. The wind felt like my parents having sex in the next room. The bus felt like a girl breaking up with me. The sky felt as though my dad was sneaking a peek at me watching mom putting the moves on the neighbor's wife while they share a floor-polish cocktail.

Am I your power lines? Are the dangling, swaying wires my nervous smile? Are the vulgar poles the buses' stale breath? Or am I just that guy who always calls you but doesn't ever seem to have much to say? Or am I simply just the observer being observed?

15. Better to be the sky—an antique, a curiosity. Better to just hang up the phone and try later. Better to just forget about it all. Better to just let it lie there and rot. Better to just let it grow old and fall apart. Better to just not even try. Better to just keep on walking, and not look it in the face. Better to not notice. Better to just forget about it. Better to just stop wondering. Better to just stop writing.

16. Now I am going inside of myself. I'm growing deeper, wider, bigger—inside of myself. Inside there's this summer, and in the summer this bus slowly disappears into the distance, over a slight hill. A bird slowly fades out of sight. The wheat is still in an endless field. A kid in an old fading jacket of mine shuffles his feet against the dust. He stops. He slowly turns to take it all in. The wind brushes him. The sun touches him. He is braver than either of us. Everything is quiet and motionless, and the fall casts its long shadow as it waits, just around the corner, in the bedroom upstairs.

car battery sex toy
(every day is a gift from God)

Part I

I quit my sex gizmo cosmetology job as today they only wanted me to take off my clothes, which comes as no surprise to me bus crash dry limp body dick. Causing a bus to crash was easy as I grabbed the wheel all men want it spinning skinny into the oncoming trucks spanking slabs of guilt trying to get by with those car battery sex toys jumping out of crash dangling limp body dick.

Work in the sex industry is about the only option secretary receptionist waitress disgruntled employee walk off the job.

[And this is the ranting, abstract, preachy part that will lose most people: Why do the media in your head, a subdivision of your subconscious, always portray really smart people with good ideas as wackos, wimps, geeks, and nerds? Goofs, slacks, dicks, clods, dweebs, buddies, petes, four-eyes, eggheads, witches, commies, fags, liberals, weirdos. We are hostages to this spoon-fed doctrine which lulls people into complacency and brainwashes them to fear the intellectuals who spend their time in libraries as opposed to wasting it in consumer shopping malls, by portraying them as unfashionably weird. Fortunately it has been proven that fashion is obsolete, as you chase your own tail throwing money after the new year, jealously trying to keep up with everyone else. They don't want you to think, is what they are saying—you must follow to be accepted, as freethinkers are weirdoes who will stay home the night of the prom. Those who are different must be feared and excluded to make the talentless feel better about themselves. And in the end, somehow, you will be the one responsible for the insecurities and jealousies of all those weaker people.]

"Sure I'm distraught," I shout as he collapses and I wander through the restaurant of our love. "Promises, promises." You only wanted my bus crash body love. Broken glass never bothered me loud ripping metal noise banter. Flying body art and loud scraping pinging crunch love. This is my art. You are entangled as it mutates beyond either of us to ripple on into future lives and proof and events yet unborn, rendering the already fragile notion of reason impotent and the concept of perception weak with shuddering envy.

The cars argued in that beautiful way, in our ripping metal whispers, tempting tempers to flair until a fight broke out. Bing bang pop crash. It was all so pretty. It was all so catchy.

You live in your organic traffic life, so I must interact with you on that level, in your own native tongue—so I must get your life to fight. I must wake you up to life. Language and knowledge and communication is what will save you. They are your best defense, your only weapons. This is my fashion, my reason. This is what's "in," what's "hot" this week. Your life is my art, I must tamper and alter. Snip, snip.

So I quit, wanting to run things—why not? I lie flying through your air and into your perceptions, hitting the sidewalk out the door through the exploding air. My life

i'm right here

floats freely, strangling your heart from behind as I steal your wallet leaving my fake name and number with you at the restaurant by your jacket that I smeared with mustard as you quickly shuffled off to some other arbitrary distraction, Mr. "Oh, I'll help you—pick a girl up at a disaster guy."

[Hey, let me tell ya somethin' pal, guys like you've been payin' my rent for years. So who's pickin' up who, Mr. Macho Man?]

I leave my life for you to think about in the stained improvisation of food smeared on fashion. I leave my lie, my seed, for you to mull over checking into a hotel room with your wallet take you out for dinner oh I've got a credit card you look shaken up gee I'm so hungry you sure do look sharp.

Cut the drapes with scissors caressing your credit cards how will I ever pay for it Mr. Manners. Pay you back it won't cost a thing. My bad day changes your life catch you in my net, wreck the TV, clog the toilet, stain the carpet, cut up the bed sheets, slash the mattress of your love—sweet credit card love Mr. Leave your wallet in your jacket as you turn to hop away coffee stain coffee grounds coffee coffee coffee coffee.

I just wanted you to remember me giggles Martin as he watches from the sidelines of my play with glee. My play, my opera, my canvas, my composition. I saw the bus as a banal purveyor of obsolete norms and conventions—a deliverer; the glass, a baptism. Martin, now nude, yet still well-behaved, saw the thing as a flower opening up, a budding of thought and reaction. The bud of technology opens up to embrace you, or swallow you. This blossoming was quite clever, yet the traditional connections of viewer to world unfortunately remained quite arbitrary. Your life is a collage of ideas that someone else accidentally pasted together. So I must take a can opener to that lie, open it up like a flower, like a torch as its flamelike petals twist to reveal, commenting on the natural beauty, and the destructive power of technology.

part II

Dave flipped the channels quickly with the remote, preferring to experience TV in that random distortion of a consumable reality while Martin made love to him. They did it on the floor, the two brothers drenched in the glow of a flickering electronic hearth. Samples flash by—believe this, buy that, you need this, you don't need that, thought is bad, ideas are worse, ideas are worse, ideas are worse, ideas, ideas, ideas.

Grinding philosophy scars, that's all anything is and it's all anything ever was, merely scar tissue of outdated ideas. Like the lineal descendants of dead cattle lumps like bright yellow suns that smell of raw eggs and wet plaster in the morning. A little jar of silverware polish can get you a long way, after all. Your life is merely ornamentation. And pointless ornamentation at that. I merely want to point that out to you. I merely want to strip it away to reveal to you. That's basically all I'm trying to do here. I'm trying to help you, and in doing so I may be able to help myself sort a few things out as well.

Dave explained his perception of the thing as experiencing an escape from the traditional dead end existence in stories like these, it is a need, an inevitability, rather than my need to control a situation.

That was all OK by me; at least they weren't reading any of their "poetry," although the gas cans and matches were staged and ready to go—a climax to their orgasm.

"People . . ." he began through his heavy breathing and thrusting, rotating his shoulders and pelvis around and around and around in tight circles, "People believe things just happen." The images flashed on them, bathing them, burning into them, staining them as the bus thrust itself deeper into the stubborn, unlubricated oncoming traffic. "What you have to decide is whether you're just rationalizing your own antisocial behavior and blaming others for your own concerns, or whether you actually stand for something productive."

Snidbits of life, all you have time for, no longer connected to their origin, dangle at my will, severed from their mother to be mixed and planted with other snidbits of ideas to grow smirking smugly. I live through docudramas, and the boys videotape my art and make love to it at their leisure, attempting to raise above the media's paranoid grip on your perceptions, on your brainwashed pea brain sinking in your flyspeck of an insignificant existence through juxtaposed associations and alienation. Alas, I am just like you, no better and no worse—but a snob, a phony, like you, as I grasp for some form of insignificant control, ducking insight for the more comfortable coma of a droning sameness. Who is better off? I think, cursed, knowing it is all futile. At least I attempt some mastery over these found urban artifacts, this urban archeology clipped from books, plagiarized, as I am a forger, a reassembler.

And I might follow you around, influencing these little happenstances. Little by little. This is how I try to find myself in the presumed coherence, balancing out my inadequacies and outcast status in confusion, not as a revenge, but using chaos as a ballet so I can sort it all out. I am a ruler, a weak king, flawed, and easy to bait and tempt with your acceptance, as you dangle it knowingly before my watery eyes, you see, yet I am also caught in the mass movement, surrendering to the environment, as if someone else were tinkering with my life, little by little, a tweak here and an adjustment there.

How can I spiritually absorb you, and you me, unless we interact? How can I balance out the ambivalence that is the condition of modern existence? I infect you with my doctrine, you are my petri dish and I use you to sort out my pesky little identity crisis, to iron out the obsolescence of realism, the futility of fragmentation, and the futility to escape the futility of life and the norms of arbitrary populism.

I squat to urinate on the floor. "Get those old tires in here, roll them in and get those gas cans over here." Lives collide and interface with the reality of broken glass and the invisible explosion of poisoned food. Vomiting in the bathroom, if he actually made it that far, jump-starts that interaction. My piss hisses like a zipper stinging the carpet. I pull up my pants and straighten up to pour some coffee down the back ventilation slots of the TV. "Maybe we should go back after that guy? I'm not sure I'm done with him just yet. This takes patience, this is an art, hurry up over there, let's rent a car and go influence some lives," I say while smearing some fecal matter on the wall and lamp shade, spreading it with his credit card as the brothers vigorously make love, violently hate-fucking one another as one of them repeats over and over "Dad liked you best, Dad liked you best."

"Hurry up, hurry up, let's go out and make a difference, let's go out and affect some lives, let's dabble in bus art and other chemistry." I said the day before the argument. So now go out and write a story about it.

an unusual occurrence
(composition #5 and #19)

    Wires spiraled from the big, gleaming helmet. He was sitting back, reclining high up in a very strange chair—mechanical gear controlling it—black vinyl, shiny knobs, wires everywhere. We burst in. I stopped in the doorway, stunned, holding the rest back and crouching tightly, pointing stiffly. I screamed, "My God! He's got it on his head!"

an unsightly act of inexpressible horror

The rag could hold only so much. I had to keep wringing it out into the bucket, the yellow juice a tangy Kool-Aid. Grandpa stood above me smiling with glee. "We finally got him... We finally got him..." he whispered over and over.

the boogeyman dangling upside down in the rafters of the garage like a big, wet coat

I notice his eyeball resting like a big gumball on the smooth, oily floor. I put my foot over it, slowly rolling it back and forth under my shoe. The shadows swung over my foot. I quietly bring it down, effortlessly applying pressure.

adventure #26

An alarm jumped just as I turned for the door. A blaze of red lights burned across the walls and the room shook. As I turned, the heavy door was blown from its hinges. I didn't so much as turn as I was thrown from the door. I felt the earth drop away from me and the room move ten feet as I spun in the air.

The floor rushed up to me and I met it by sliding across it on my chest. As I tried to get up, I saw people running back and forth through the thin haze of gray smoke. The room seemed to be moving, tilting to the left, then quickly falling away to the right.

I tried to grip the floor and roll over. Some little people scurried by, two or three hurdled me and some more hopped clear of me on pogo sticks, only to be lost in the fog of smoke.

I heard commotion, pandemonium, coughing, yelling, and the unmistakable "ka-ching ka-ching" of a few odd pogo sticks. And I knew it, right then I knew. Terror swept over me, pounding in my chest, filling me like wet cement. It was Jean-Claude's genetically engineered monkey-men lawyers. They had tracked me down like a dog. And now they had burst in.

i'm right here

I had heard of such a brigade, stories about them uttered only in the late of night—oh, such terrible stories. Tales of genetically engineered monkey-men lawyers with eighteenth century names, with fairy tale names—Nehemiah, Malachi, Aloicious—resentful divorce lawyers, embittered salesmen, acrobatic monkey-men, biting, kicking, hissing, spitting monkey-men. Mean suckers—one and all.

I tried to get up but caught a pogo stick in the back from out of nowhere. My back curled and I felt as though I had swallowed my tongue. Four of them grabbed me. I screamed but no one answered. It was muffled by the confusion and pain that swam up my sides. They grabbed me off the floor—one at each arm and leg, bringing to stark raving life my worst fear—that of being accosted by a gang of lawyers.

They dragged me toward the door. I tried to wiggle free, but their little grips were impressively tight. I began screaming like a child—kicking, hissing, spitting for help. "Nnnooooooo!" What did they want from me? Why were they taking me? What were they going to do with me?

My head struggled frantically, searching for help as they dragged me closer and closer to the hall, but all I found was smoke and the grainy silhouettes of people running, little people in tight striped T-shirts with their names on the fronts and backs in thin black letters—Cornelius and Boris—and the lost outlines of technicians in lab coats, frantically swinging mops and squeegees and ladders in the thin gray steam of smoke. I saw Elvis's head slosh up to the glass with a concerned look spreading across his planet of a face like the changing of the seasons, his eyes slowly scanning back and forth to follow from the golden liquid.

Some monkey-men emerged from the darkness of the hall, scampering past me toward the tank. They loped along, dragging cameras and video gear. Oh my God, they were here for Elvis! My God, they were here for the King!

adventure #26

Fear stripped away all I had known. I remember hearing stories that the other side was a part of our government too—an opposing faction, another side, another army who were working on the stuff too—the Elvis stuff, the fountain of youth stuff, the UFO stuff, stuff they'd make you disappear for. I'd heard it so many times I didn't even notice it anymore—a mistrust of it all. And now suddenly here I was floating in it.

The heavy door was lying on the floor about ten feet from the entrance. As we entered the darkness of the tunnel, my panic flooded over to become me. I reached out, wiggling my hand to try to grab the wall, to try to grab the light, to pull myself back in. I drowned in the darkness, screaming insanely, uncontrollably, until suddenly one of the monkey-men let go of my arm and my shoulder dropped to the pavement with a sharp thud. The monkey-man fell away and slammed against the wall. I turned just in time to see a technician stab the one holding my other arm square between the eyes, recoiling, then slashing him across the jaw with a broken broom handle. Splinters of wood drifted down on me as my other shoulder hit the ground.

I kicked and twisted frantically to loosen their grip on my legs, buy their hairy hands bit into me like tiny vices. I kicked one free as another technician joined the assault, swinging a short rubber hose in one hand and a bucket with the other. It was an impressive one-two combination. The technician wielding the stick cracked one of the monkey-men below the knee and again under the chin. The simian fell back with the blow and limped as he assumed a karate stance, then kicked with both feet in a scissors action, then crouched tightly as the technician dropped the broom and collapsed to his knees, enthusiastically clutching his crotch with both

i'm right here

hands. The broom handle *clacked* as it bounced on the concrete. He sang an "Oooooooo" out of a tight pucker as he shuffled across the hall on his kneecaps. "Jesus, Mary, and Joseph," he moaned.

I rolled to get clear of the melee, fumbling for the stick and finally popping to my feet as the other technician swirled his weapons back and forth in propeller motions to cover me.

One of the monkey-men began to rise from the floor, shaking his head. I turned and whacked him furiously in every manner available, but it didn't seem to faze him. He rose as I thrashed his back and sides and clubbed his head in frantic, hollow clucking sounds that faded in gasps of suffocation in the damp hall.

The other technician shuffled over on his knees, still gripping his crotch. He cupped his privates with one hand and reached down into his lab coat with the other. As the monkey-man collected himself, the technician reached over and zapped him with a little black box that looked like a television remote. The simian shook for a moment, his white eyes rolling back into his head in the heartbreakingly dim light. He looked at me as he shook. He looked right into me, right through me. The technicians watched down the hall as this one, single monkey-man held my attention in his grip. He reached to me, his little hairy arm quivering. His eyes grew bigger and he moaned to me: "Remember . . . Remember what it's like to live . . . Remember." Then he backpedaled, hit the wall, and slid to the floor, his body empty of life as it folded in on itself.

I turned and saw the technician with the bucket kicking another monkey-man in the head. He had both of the monkey-men down and incapacitated, the dented bucket lying at his feet, the hose wrapped snugly around the other monkey's stocky neck.

adventure #26

I helped one technician to his feet and we pulled the other back into the room. "Sorry about that," the one who took the shots to the groin huffed as he limped. "We had to stall until they all got inside," he shrugged. "We didn't want any getting away." He reached over and fell against me. I caught him and propped him up as the murky light of the room blessed us.

He pointed that small black wand across the room and a gray concrete panel in the wall slid up. There was a strange pause, and I knew something was going to happen. There was this sensation, everything slowed, shadows ripped in that secret passage, a commotion of shadows fought, and suddenly a group of ostriches burst out, appearing from the grainy smoke like spirits, galloping madly, wildly shaking their heads and twisting their bodies, flopping their feathers, flapping their wings. Some let out blood curdling screeches that rung in the air, echoing, shaking the room, splitting my ears.

They charged, legs kicking, stringy necks undulating. A monkey-man loped from the smoke and clubbed the technician in my arms on the back of the neck. He went limp and fell out of my grip, slumping to the floor. The simian cocked his weapon back to strike me. I turned away. As I raised my arm, he was obliterated by an ostrich—just trampled out of sight. An ostrich caught another one low and lifted to fling him high in the air. Another monkey-man stepped out of the smoke at me, but turned as he saw another charging ostrich from the corner of his eye. He set his stance and karate-chopped the large bird square between the eyes, dropping it to the floor in a heap. Another ostrich appeared from behind him, whipping its neck to swing its head and knock him off his feet. He slipped to the ground and the ostrich began pecking the hell out of his face and skull and hands, jackhammer fast, as the monkey-man tried to cover himself. It was a brutal sight, blood squirting and limbs flailing as a *thatch thatch thatch* noise turned my stomach.

Sickened, I grimaced and turned to duck away, gliding low across the floor to grip a wall and stay clear. I surveyed the area, gulping and breathing hard as I rubbed the clammy floor and wall with my palms.

I watched other ostriches claw with their powerful legs. The ugly sight gripped me. I can't explain it—the smell of Elvis's algae—that stagnant-lake-on-a-hot-sunny-day smell being overwhelmed by blood and heat and smoke and the bleach and ammonia of cleaning supplies.

Ostriches and technicians and little monkey people lay scattered like dried leaves. But I had no sympathy for them. That was the only thing I felt—just that. It was suddenly all that simple. Suddenly I had no sympathy for any of them. I was numb, utterly empty of feeling. Let them drown in it all. I heaved and huffed, out of breath. I strained to see Elvis through the smoke. Our eyes met. And all I could think was, "Man, Elvis, you stink."

The monkeys began to pick themselves up, to roll over and help one another to the door. Some stood by the doorway as cover while others limped out. Suddenly I caught a large, cycloptic gorilla-man lurch into the hall from out of the gray fog. A group of technicians quickly followed the hulking beast.

I couldn't believe this. I couldn't understand it. I looked around and there were maybe three or four monkeys slumped about, lying on the floor or against the wall. A technician ran back in from the hall, stopped, and skidded on the floor. "They're taking off on their jet packs!" he screamed. "They're getting away!"

adventure #26

The other technicians picked themselves up and began limping toward the door. Again, the ostriches rushed out of their tunnel in a flurry—a flood of clean black and white feathers and long necks riding snakelike legs. The technicians circled their arms in windmill motions to signal them out and down the tunnel. Then some giraffes came running out too. They galloped freely, kicking up their long legs in the tall room. They circled the room, impressively kicking up dust in a collective herd. I looked over and saw that Elvis was pleased, amused even—as if this were a circus they performed for him from time to time—like he knew what was up, as if saying, "Go get 'em boys."

With the King's silent approval, the ostriches and giraffes circled the room, picking up steam. The technicians ran around in that circle, each grabbing a long neck, and swinging themselves onto a back with a running jump.

I stepped from the wall in confused disbelief. An ostrich circled around, zooming with such fierce velocity I couldn't get out of the way. I couldn't move. I turned my back to avoid the crash, pivoting around and covering my head with my arms. I felt its long neck zipping low between my legs and scooping me up onto its soft back in one running motion. Instinctively I gripped its feathers as we circled the room, suddenly shooting into the darkness.

I looked back over my shoulder as I rode, undulating forward and back. I watched the last of Elvis's faint, ghostly face disappear through the fog. And I felt him inside of me, warming me, as if saying: "I'll always be with you."

We flew down the hall, the wind rushing through my hair, beating my face, deafening my ears, hurting my eyes as I bobbed. The hall was dark but didn't seem long, due to our speed. We rushed magically up the labyrinth of stairs and out into the blinding heat of day. We raced across a small parking lot and shot through a field of golden grass.

I hunched low, my legs clamped tight in a riding manner. I looked to see the other technicians beside me and ahead, riding the beasts, thundering ahead, thundering on, necks stretching, thighs churning.

Up ahead some began to slow and dismount. Mine slowed as we approached them. I slid off its back and looked around as a strange whooshing sound filled the air. I turned to see the genetically engineered monkey-men lawyers floating away from the abandoned air base. They were gliding on the wind, ten feet above the ground as if surfing on their bellies, their jet packs singing a slick *whoooo-sheeee-whooooo* sound.

They roared with serious faces. We could only watch as they glided in formation, disappearing into the distance. The lone helicopter from the base fluttered vainly after them.

The silver chain-link fence was up ahead, maybe fifty feet, but we didn't try for it. The ostriches looked about and huddled; some bent down and ate grass. The giraffes wandered over to the tree-line. "We've got a call out to the air force," one of the redneck technicians mentioned. "No, no, they're gone," another lamented softly as he shuffled the soil under his feet. "Come on, we've got a lot of work to do," another muttered as he turned back.

I looked over at the one beside me and asked, "Did we win?"

He looked at me and then returned his attention to the dots disappearing over the trees in the hazy blue distance. He ran his hand over the top of his slick, black hair. He sucked in the deep air, then exhaled, squinting. "Soon," he sighed. "Soon enough."

dinner one night

Sigmund Freud stopped over for dinner last night. We had hot dogs and pickles—some bananas too. I didn't touch a bite, as I was afraid to even move.

some more words that remind me of you

    Remember that one time when I was sad and you kissed me on the lips in front of strangers while all the world bloomed with effortless nature and sentiment like a burning goat herd on a vast beach that grew fingers of sleeping dogs with dreams of you like crisp white sheets flapping on the clothesline in the deep grass when I was growing up as a kid in our little fenced-in sandbox of a back yard that I pretended was a long beach?

1000 stories

ecuador

"How was your day, honey? Did you have a good day?"
"Yes, actually, I had a great day. A great day indeed—every last bit of it. Everyone was very polite, for once. Every last person. Imagine that."
"Oh my, well, that is a real treat. I know how much that means to you. Were you productive? Did you end up getting a lot done?" (wringing hands on apron)
"Oh . . . no . . . not much . . . No, not much at all . . . Not in the least . . . But everyone was painfully polite for a change—and that's what counts." (He unstraps his cumbersome flamethrower and clumsily lowers it to the floor, leaning it against the pantry wall, next to his rain shoes. He rests the nozzle on the tanks.)

Several blocks away, a monkey escapes from the zoo. After curiously wandering the alleys for a while, it finally climbs a tree in their back yard. It stands on a branch and hops up and down, loudly slapping itself on the head twenty-five times in a very immature, self-referential manner. It does this as if to say: "Hey everybody, look at me, look at me—I'm a monkey!"

i'm right here

    Several blocks away, a truck loaded with bananas skids in the rain and tumbles off a high bridge. It spins slowly, like a giant feather, end over end as it falls, finally landing upside down in the rocky creek below, damming the trickle of water.

    Some beavers eat the bananas (the truck had split down the middle); as if in time twenty-five of them would eventually begin to exhibit human qualities, hijacking a phone company truck, and demanding tailors.

    It took the zoo personnel an hour to notice that Ju-Ju had wandered off. They rushed into the streets, each hurrying in a different direction.

    Peter huffed down a tree-lined alley, as if to plead: "Please don't forget me. Please, please, don't ever forget me." He carried a tool belt (several of the tools were missing), which, at first sight, seemed to represent the love and understanding we all feel toward our fellow man.

    Lucy ran down the block and ducked into the park, head darting, eyes searching, as if to declare: "Oh my God. Oh my savior in heaven above I'm going to die alone. I don't want to die alone." She wore a greasy hair net—which symbolized, in the broadest of terms, her hypochondria and perpetual need for adulation.

    Desmond hopped on a city bus to sneak off to his favorite bar for a quick nip, as if to proclaim: "There's a whole 'nother world out there, babe. Many worlds. All glowing with tiny possibilities." He carried a flask in his vest pocket, which stood for the freedom and power deeply nested in each of us. His pompadour represented complete and total victory over all his rivals.

    Ethel calmly walked around the perimeter, as if to point out: "When I get home I'm gonna strap on my leather

ecuador

boots and go out into the back yard and dig me a really deep hole to sit in." She clung to a cattle prod, illustrating her vulnerable, nurturing side.

Benny stayed behind to tend to the other primates, as if to say: "Wow, look at the titties on that gorilla." He stared in awe, hands free, indicating he was open to new views about the world.

"By the way, I'm leaving you for a man from Ecuador..." She stood before him in the pantry, still wringing her hands in her apron (while everyone else seemed to be lost out there, still searching for their own lost monkeys).

Suddenly he began to see her flicker before his eyes, as if fading out of sight, like a lost country. Her thin green eyes became its lost rivers; her pale narrow chin was its forever mountains; her flush cheeks, its misplaced golden valleys; her thick eyebrows, its missing clouds; her beautiful, smooth hair, its lapse of imagination; her stunning smile, the deprivation of its skies; her tender skin, the forfeiture of its soft grass; her quiet stares, the dispossession of its sunny days; her supple touches, the wasting of its vast oceans; her lithesome yawns, its irretrievable snowy peaks; her infinite patience, its unspoken-for forests; her gentle whisper, the squandering of its wind; her mysterious mouth, its forgotten monkeys in trees.

He stood silently, sipping his martini, looking through her, searching for that country, hoping for its soft skies, wishing for its feathery golden grass, longing for its monkeys in trees.

"He's a midget-wrestling banana importer from Ecuador. From the village of Babahoyo. I'm leaving you for him. I'm sorry."

i'm right here

"Oh, yes, well, that does sound intriguing. I'm... I'm sorry to hear that. That's very disappointing news..." (he seemed to stagger back a step) (he put a finger up to his mouth) (he didn't know what to say) "...By the way, your hair looks very very nice done up that way." (He looked out the window, out at the new garbage cans leaning against the garage like shining silver prayers. He looked out the window ... and ... and ... and ... thought about pulling the godforsaken map from the utility drawer.)

She turned and reached for the door. "Please don't go!" he blurted and she stopped for a moment, pausing as the monkey outside slapped itself on the head and vehemently waved its arms, like a... like a... like a warning.

In his mind he could picture her turn her head slightly and softly say something like "I have to" and gently step out the door.

"You kick ass," he whispered, as if thinking out loud. "You kick so much ass," he admitted as he looked down at the baby blue tile floor between them. She turned and lunged for him, wrapping her arms around him. "Oh I love you," she whispered. And as they spun around in a great embrace, he noticed, looking out the window that the monkey was gone— not in the branches, not anywhere. And that's when he saw a naked man running off with one of their new garbage cans.

her name is radriva pasternak; perhaps you know her

part I

I've got it tucked under my arm, yet, due to its heft and girth, it's safe from the unmotivated, drizzly rain.
I don't mind the rain, not today. I got that 400,000-page love letter tucked under my arm. The fucker's the size of the motherlovin' phone book. I wrote it on newsprint—took me three months, day and night. I got it all in there—every last thought of her. I have to hold it up with both arms lest it go limp under its own ambition. They should *sell* books like this.
I've got on my belt of old watches, each one hooked together like a chain. And I've got on two of my five-dollar trench coats—two of the good plaid ones. They still smell like the men who died in them.
I got them where I got some of the other good ones, at that secondhand store out by all the junkyards, the one on the dirt road lined with those long, tall fences of oily wood planks and rusting, gray corrugated metal. The ones with the bathtubs leaning against them, lined up all the way down the block like coffins, and refrigerators milling about in rows like

i'm right here

graves, like defeated soldiers with weeds separating their disinterested ranks.

That secondhand shop is in an old wood building, a long, thin one, with peeling paint, deep sand for a parking lot, a sagging, leaky roof, and clothes with notebook paper pinned to the lapels and sleeves. These notes tell of the owners, who they were and how they died. They are carefully written letters—arduously, clumsily so, written by a child. They are just modest notes, several sentences, yet with perfect spelling. They are pinned to all these sad shirts of weak yellow and fearful brown, large lapels, and cowboy-like pockets. The leisure suits are mostly moldy brown or powder blue. The punks love 'em, they gobble 'em up, but then again they're pretty sophisticated 'round these parts. They know a good suit when they see one.

As for me, well, bury me in one of those red velvet suits with the big silky ruffles. Bury me with an 8" x 10" photo of David Cassidy. Or bury me in my Travis "Machine Gun" Grant's basketball uniform—the number 42, yellow with red trim from the '73-'74 San Diego Conquistadors of the old ABA.

When I'm in there, in that place of places, sometimes I wonder what's going to happen to my clothes when I move on. I don't dwell on it, though; it'll come soon enough. That's what my calculations show—that's what I've gauged. So I try to think about other possibilities—of love—giant love, simple love, love to share clean lawns of grass and still, gentle, shallow lakes with the calm, patient sky of her eyes. That sort of love, nothing fancy.

If you go there, leave your dreams out in the hot parking lot, or better yet, kid, don't even bring them along at all—leave them at home where they belong. You don't want

to show them up to the careful, deliberate people who go in there. You wouldn't want to rub their noses in it.
 You'd be busy enough in there anyway. It's a great place to get fishbowls. I musta got a ton of 'em there, all of them solid and full, with beautiful crystal lives. I've got 'em lined up at eye level on a perfect pine shelf along one wall of my living room. The other wall has another 1" x 10" pine shelf with old irons lined up like prayers. I've got 'em standing up on end, like those rows of bathtubs and refrigerators. I polish their swollen silver to a blinding shine. I hang their thick cloth cords down behind the shelf. It's a truly astounding display. I try to keep them alive, the way a hunter mounts a deer or a pheasant, so they will always be safe with them.
 I got a lot of good paperbacks there too—a lot of old dime-store books that I stuffed in a black bookshelf in the hall—one with glass doors and the ornament of a cathedral. That's about it for furniture as far as the living room and hallway go, though. Come on by sometime, we'll hang out for a while. There's nothing else out here. Nothing but the sky and the edge of town. The sky is my favorite thing. The edge of town is nice, too.

part II

 I'll see her for maybe an hour a week—like a television show that I'll turn on. Or maybe I am a television show that she turns on. I'll call her and we'll go for walks and talk about the past in dictation her simple skies would be proud of, in terms that will bring the complicated grass to tears, to the eventual tears of the shyly rising sun. And somehow that magic hour will keep me going through the week, until I get the courage to call and call until I finally reach her again.

i'm right here

Her name is Radriva Pasternak; perhaps you know her. Perhaps you know her from some other where. Perhaps you can mention me to her, perhaps you'll tell her about me, put in a good word for me. Perhaps you know people who are in her good favor, or have sat next to her on the bus or stood in line waiting to get into a club somewhere.

I've been thinking about telling her how I feel. I've been thinking about it a lot lately; in fact, I even wrote her a love letter, a pretty long one. I've been thinking of trimming it down some—I wouldn't want her to think I was obsessing about her or being nutty or anything. I've been distilling it from over 400,000 pages down to just one sentence. It's so hard to pick the right words. And it's about the only permanent thing I have—feelings, feelings like this.

Maybe it's better to drop it, let it burn away, rust and fade in the sun. If I drop it all on her it may take her by surprise and crush the friendship. But then again it might just open up something wonderful.

Somehow just knowing her I see things differently. At least I could get to know her. At least I could know her for those handfuls of random hours and all those months spent writing. At least I could know her there in my perfect dreams and sentimental writing. At least I could know her for a little while.

I wrote this extensive 400,000-page love letter to her—just as *War and Peace* was probably a love letter Leo Tolstoy wove to someone he knew briefly in his youth.

After it was completed and I reread it, I decided it was best not to give it to her. It will just be better that way—what if she laughs at it or won't carry it to where she is going and finally just ends up forgetting it on some bench in a really bad part of town and it gets all rained on, the newsprint arching to bubble uncomfortably and finally I will end up tripping *her name is radriva pasternak*

over it years from now, somehow remembering it through the fog of time. And I will have to stand above it there on the sidewalk as it holds the flimsy wooden screen door to an old auto parts store open in some forgotten small town that was magic once, or that at least one time long ago had some type of potential or vocation leaning toward magic.

And I'd be standing above it, looking down at it in a puddle of mud and gas, holding the hand of your child and all the way back home I'd have to tell him about love as all the tall stalks of corn filed by.

Maybe she'll find it at the foot of her door, where I plan to leave it. Maybe she'll think it is the new phone book and put it where she keeps her old phone book and then one day weeks later, or perhaps months even, she will pull it out when she needs to look something up and she will open it and discover it is not a phone book at all—not in the least, and she will begin to read it in puzzled curiosity, forgetting her other appointments that day. Maybe she'll blow off that entire week even. Maybe after she reads the whole thing she'll track me down and find me. She might ring my bell late at night, just as she finishes it, just as she finishes a box of really dry crackers, and she'll get up and dust the crumbs from its thin, dry, crinkly pages, and she'll stomp across town and ring my bell and I'll open my door, looking frazzled and worn and blinking from the bare bulb high up in the sandy parking lot, and I will see her standing in her bathrobe and she will arch her back and hurl that heavy sucker around at me, kind of sidearm and kind of shot-put style. And I'll catch that thing right in the breadbasket, my arms curling to clutch it as it folds and rolls and wiggles. And she'll address me as "You bastard!" and then stomp off, across town, back to her place.

No thank you, I say. I'd just rather hold it here for a while—all 400,000 pages, all carefully chosen from all the

i'm right here

words available anywhere, from all possible thoughts imaginable, all misspelled with Calvinistic love and treasure—a castle of words to live in.

Here I am, standing in the rain. My arms are getting tired now. I don't want it around anyway, not cluttering up my place, not in the garage or garden or anywhere. It belongs to her. I've thought about it for a long time now. I'll bring it to her when I know she's not around. I'll leave it on her doorstep. It'll be the first thing she sees when she gets home. It'll probably just get thrown away anyway—let's hope she's had a good day at work.

But then I think again—maybe I'll toss it in a garbage can. If it were going to happen, it would've already started by now. I wonder now, if she's nothing more than some pleasant residue from a nice dream—a vague dream that I seem to have fond memories of. Then I reconsider and think maybe I'll keep it for a little while longer. But then I think about it again, I smile and think, what the hell, we're all gonna die soon enough anyway.

the promise

"I said I'd be back when I made something of myself."
Those words lingered, sticking to the cold air as she blinked, trying to remember me. I pulled down my hood with two fingers and shook my head. "I said I'd be back when I made something of myself." I repeated calmly. "I know, my hair was different back then, I mean four years is a long time I guess, but then again it really isn't all that long." I had to stop myself from rambling. I had to bite my tongue not to interrupt. I couldn't believe it was her.

She just stood there blinking and squinting, trying to find my face back there in her past—or at least trying to locate someone who had the same shape and general Christian features as myself.

"I moved in next door to you about two-and-a-half years ago," I said, trying to draw some saliva to lubricate my nervous words in the dry air. "Yeah, I moved in next to you—into that brown brick building—into a shitty little cavelike place that had an old stove that hissed loudly, keeping me away from the sting of gas that clouded in the kitchen. I didn't cook for months." I shook my head and then shrugged deeply. "I tried to make a lot of noise to see if you would come and knock on my door, or at least call the police and send them in

i'm right here

your place, as I was too shy to knock on yours. I'd play my old Black Sabbath tapes as loudly as I could—until the walls shook and windows rattled, but you never answered." I swallowed hard. "The Sabbath wasn't working, it just made me depressed and impotent after a while."

She pursed her lips and nodded with a serious, yet warm and compassionate look.

"Well, most of it was OK . . ." I leaned in. ". . . The album *Sabbath Bloody Sabbath* was the only *really* depressing one."

She nodded with an "Oh, sure" look of friendly but serious understanding—as if she knew that that was a particularly challenging piece to try to "rock out" to.

"Anyway," I continued, ". . . I went to a seminar in the room next to the people who wet the bed, and things are mostly better in that area now."

The wind blew loudly against us, its thick gusts causing me to raise my voice. She had to lean in a little closer.

"Maybe it was the apartment—as dark and unforgiving as winter." I caught myself as I thought I was rambling. "Anyway . . ." I restarted. ". . . I went away and got an education, as you weren't interested in me back then, and now I'm back and have a respectable job, attend services sharply every bright Sunday morning, and have plants and fish and a dog and nice clothes and a bright apartment that I keep very clean, with a clean sink and a clean shower and a pleasant smelling hamper. I can cook, sort of, and kind of speak a foreign language and am trying to teach myself guitar, although I must admit I'm not that good at it yet as I have been busy with a lot of other stuff." I swallowed again. "I don't sit and couch in front of the electric god—nor, similarly, do I stay out late with any shiftless posers or bandwagoneers. And I've grown my hair long because I know *the promise*

you always were into that. Moreover I've got an ear full of earrings, an old leather jacket, an old European motorcycle, and a goatee. Furthermore, I don't lie, cheat, steal, do drugs, boss people around, listen to country western, wear lifts, or worship Satan. Nor do I associate with those who do," I nodded dramatically. "I'm a respectable citizen who participates in each election—even the minor local ones. I give three hours a week to charity and write my mother and grandmother when I can, although mostly the same things happen to me over and over without anything really new to break it all up." I inhaled deeply. "So you can *plainly* see that it is *clearly* obvious that I am indeed more than qualified to go out with you now."

We looked at each other for a quick moment, I with a hopeful, optimistic expression—one I'd earned through years of work, through tough days and doubts—fighting opinions counter to my own beliefs, dredging through financial hardships, dead-end jobs with horrible bosses wearing horrifying lives, and dank places to live with bitchy, lying roommates who cough into your peanut butter, who fart deep into your ice cream, and evil girlfriends, to finally make it up this mountain, to finally crawl up to the light of day, to finally crawl up to her.

"I said I'd be back when I made something of myself and here I am," I spat as I heaved and breathed hard.

She just looked at me with her thin mouth slightly ajar. Then finally the corners of her mouth began to stir, and turn. And she slowly nodded as she squinted, still trying to make me out, shuffling through all her old stuff back there. She slowly nodded and drawled deeply, "Oooohhh hiiii . . . hooow've you been?" and smiled slightly as another guy came up from behind them. He was wearing these brightly colored, though slightly fading, road-map pajamas and he clomped along in bright red cowboy boots. A little kid's red plastic

i'm right here

cowboy hat with thick white stitching around its brim balanced on his head. It barely fit, just sitting there up in that saddle of hair, riding on his head. His hair was big—blow-dried to feather back in a late-'70s disco style.

And then another guy stepped up, but hung back a little—standing behind them, impatiently looking in the other direction. He was wearing a staggeringly foul powder-blue polyester leisure suit with matching thick white belt and white shoes with big brass buckles. Under the astounding suit he wore an orange T-shirt that advertised in thin red marker: "Eddie has a tiny penis." I wasn't sure what that was all about, but glad I didn't ask.

He was sporting a wig—a dishwater-blond shaggy Rod-Stewart-1974-rooster type. A stunning pair of 1973 aviator/Gloria Steinem-type sunglasses, the kind with the sarcastic piss-golden tint, completed the ensemble. Oh yeah, another thing was that his fly was down. Now I'm not just talkin' half-mast here—I'm talkin' way down, like the entire city was starin' right down into a full-blown yawn here. I mean I'm talkin' a full-fledged medical emergency ragin' right here, screamin' at us even. And he had this sick, blah orange shirt hangin' outta it like a tongue. Then I look over at the other guy—the cowboy—and he's got the same thing goin' down.

She wore a fringed brown suede jacket and a T-shirt that begged in thin red marker: "What is the sound of no hands clapping?"

"Hi, how ya doin', hello," I waved politely, but the cowboy just stared right through me, his eyes glazing over. The 1974 Rod Stewart guy glanced at me, then turned his attention back down the block.

"Oh, he can't talk to you," she jumped in. "He's been bad. I've got him on probation. I won't let him speak today." She did not indicate which one of them was being disciplined.

"Yeah, well, I understand." I nodded. "I grew up in a house full of women, so it's probably a wonder that I'm actually a heterosexual."

The cowboy looked down at his shoes with a shameful expression. And that's when I noticed his tattoo. "Wow," I said and sort of half pointed.

"Yep . . . every chapter, every word of *Catcher in the Rye*," She explained. "All over his body."

"Wow." I exhaled again, following the tiny words down his neck as they disappeared into his road map pajamas.

"He's got the complete formula for the hydrogen bomb running down his back." She pointed to the other guy. "Including the annotations—which run across his hairy white ass."

He kind of smirked and shrugged with pride and embarrassment. The cowboy turned and tapped his arm and they both stepped off the curb.

"Where ya goin'? You guys wanna get somethin' ta eat or somethin'? Or ya wanna go to a . . ."

"Nice ta see ya again, I gotta go," she sort of lazily half waved as she turned to join her friends.

I don't know if either of them was her boyfriend or not—or if she was the type to have a boyfriend. It was probably too impolite to ask. All I knew was they looked so free, so fresh, so bright—so alive. I wanted to go with them— the way I'm drawn to her—but they just slided on casually, too casual for me.

"Who's that?"

"Mmm, not sure."

They sulked away, moping across the street, and mumbled so slowly that I couldn't make out any of their words.

all the beautiful women

All the beautiful women in the world don't know my name. The most beautiful girl I've ever seen in all my life works at a greeting card shop downtown. She doesn't know my name.

One day I was in there standing at their newsstand and flipping through an old sports magazine from 1972 that had a sprawling, majestic color photo spread of Don Horn handing off to Donny Anderson and then to Floyd Little, spread out over about ten pages that all the eight-year-old boys would dream of and all the young girls would fall in love with.

The photo spread emerged from the pages as I melted into it. It drew me in and wrapped itself around me as I stood there on the sidelines holding a clipboard in my arms and got a hot dog up in the stands and hoped she would come over to talk to me on the sidelines there in that opera. But she didn't approach me and that frustrated me, to not be Don Horn shining there handing off to Donny or Floyd and to not have her there with me watching and wondering about me as she went about her business.

The next day I was in there again and looking at another old sports magazine from 1972. I didn't see her around. She wasn't anywhere in there.

This magazine had a wimpy postage stamp of a photo that I had to squint at to make out Jerry LeVias in his heart-stoppingly stunning pale purple-blue uniform and white helmet rising up above the cloud of a field as if a ballerina on a thin silky string, stretching out to reach God's fingers.

You could see his eyes, as big as suns, praying as they looked up to heaven to find God as Jerry reached to catch the bright blue day, and all the things I could never touch.

I know how he felt, because when I talk to her I feel like I'm talking to God. I stutter and stumble in her presence, I fall as if seeking some assistance, some guidance from her eyes. I see her in that tiny photo of Jerry LeVias. I see her as all the beautiful women in the world.

I figured it was enough that I had to parade around in that insipid costume I had to wear to work, that maybe she'd come around and see fit to have some small measure of mercy on me while I stammered and was fixing to try my best to muster something gallant from deep down inside some mystical, medieval storage room way down inside myself to call up to try and speak to her.

I was standing there, but she didn't show up. She didn't appear from her perfect place behind the counter, as if she was hiding behind tall castle walls that were twenty feet thick with cold, hard stones. She wasn't in any of her other perfect places—stocking shelves or fixing displays or toweling herself off in the morning or caressing her long, straight Thumbelina hair with her warm, perfect hands.

So I asked the guy at the counter, a tall, thin guy with a big egg face, where she was that day. I said where's that really really pretty long-haired girl today? I walked up to him

i'm right here

slowly, up to those castle gates carefully, as quietly as Jerry LeVias whispered to God in my hands and divine miracles poured out: Willie Mays's last at bat, Richard Brautigan on a wood dock, lost in a morning mist of fog.

I walked up to the castle cautiously to talk to one of its guards. He had a very casual manner about him, as if he were really somewhere else. He was a good soldier, I could tell.

I started in and he just looked sort of puzzled, as if he had never heard of anyone this beautiful in all his travels. I described her, hoping he would read my actions and mention if she had a boyfriend or not. Perhaps she was out with him, strolling on the beach or saving orphans from a fire. I was hoping he would catch on and mention where she was and who she was with so I wouldn't have to show my hand and ask. And after I was done, after I had approached her altar, all he could say was no, that she wasn't here. So I asked him the big question, as if hopelessly joining a procession of a thousand other guys throughout history, dressed in the white robes of monks, all of us brothers carrying the crush. I asked quietly, I asked him her name. I was afraid I'd go blind at that mere mention of it, maybe deaf, maybe get struck down by lightning as he uttered it, maybe that ceiling would blow away, the tiles dissipating into churning clouds at the wondrous sound of her name. And he stood there silently for that long passing moment that fathers don't tell their sons about, just that one moment when time stands still, light and sound pulling to escape its grip and all those clouds of ceiling swirling nervously, pacing suspiciously—all at the thought of her name.

I asked him her name and he looked over to some things she had stacked on a display and all he could say was *oh, her.* I asked him what her name was again and he just shrugged and said that she really didn't have one.

all the beautiful women

So I just stood there in front of him, across the desert of a counter, alone and lost out there with the cold, empty wind swirling around my legs, so far from her I wanted to die. I stood there stranded in embarrassment because I didn't have anything to purchase or any other reason to be standing there but for her, and here she goes and pulls something like this on me. Why don't you know her name? I finally snapped. *I don't know*, he said as he fiddled with his arms bent under the counter, *why does it matter?* Well, you work here, I would think you'd be smart enough to know her name. *Well, I don't.* Well, I think you'd be smart enough to know her name that's all. *Well, I'm smart enough to know it gives her the creeps you comin' around here!*

I just stood there like a monument to hope, hopin' she'd be along to open those doors to her land of comfort and beauty. But somehow I felt that she had left me hanging there, like a skinned animal, as if she liked to handle these things this way. My face started to burn red and suddenly the comfortable smell of that place began to stir in its sting. Hey, I was jus' tryin' to be friendly, that's all! I snapped as I turned away. I started moving back and slowly turned and moved down the aisle to the glass doors. I was so numb I didn't notice, betrayed by gravity, like I wasn't even walking at all, like I was just moving somehow. There was a big canister of pencils by the door, and a stack of things waiting to be shelved. As I neared it, I stepped on top of some candy boxes, crunching them down. Then cranked up and gave that pencil can a mighty kick, sending it flying end over end out the door. It spun down the hall, spilling its guts.

Perhaps she is beautiful inside there, I once thought. Like a rose in a glass vase—I can only see her reflected from behind the glass of the windows. But perhaps she is not so

i'm right here

beautiful, or just not yet anyway. Maybe she's hard and cold and unknowing in these matters, like she doesn't know how to do it all so warm and pleasant and nice—or maybe she's just afraid to open herself up to all that. Maybe she's really not all that beautiful after all, or maybe just not yet anyway. Perhaps we have yet to learn how.

I remember you

I remember when we would page through my Asian mail-order bride catalogs together and she would drift asleep and I would wake her by biting her big toe. I remember when we would watch the elementary school sexual orientation filmstrips and hygiene flicks made for the eleven-and twelve-year-olds, together in the deep wetness of the night, the projector's clicking echo haunting the walls with an impending heaviness, as if it were tapping inside my chest.

Do you remember breaking out the video camera, that lovely instrument, and taping our lovemaking while watching another tape of ourselves making love? We'd tape ourselves making love while watching ourselves making love on the big TV. Then we'd tape ourselves making love while watching the tape of ourselves making love to the tape of ourselves making love to the tape of ourselves making love to the tape.

Then we'd go to work with all ten of our TVs glowing in the townhouse windows, broadcasting our intimacy in the dark winter morning, sharing our love, boasting about it, our tumbling triple love glowing in blurry, flickering pulses—

undulating thick wrestling holds, Catholic positions, Japanese positions, American educational system positions, boring positions, dangerous athletic positions, in the silvery gray mornings, squinting through the lazy clouds.

And there you are every night, when I wake and find you at my side, gazing up at me from the worn and fading cover of an old *Life* magazine.

editorial

"She doesn't deserve a man like you!" shouted the skinny mailman at the house as he marched on down the sidewalk. "You should let him do what he wants! Let him find himself—let him grow wings!" he shouted at the next house. The house after that was hard to see as it was thickly overgrown with trees and bushes, so he looked as though he was just yelling at a tree: "I don't see why he even bothers to write you anymore!"

Liza knew there was going to be trouble when she heard him coming up the block. "Not this guy again," she whispered, then turned and headed for the garage. He was getting together some letters. A garden rake met his shins and he toppled chest first onto the smooth, hard sidewalk. The "whack" of the rake-handle-to-shin echoed excitedly in the dry morning air, wiggling on like a snake. She dropped the rake and scrambled out of the bushes on her hands and knees, stopping to pick up one letter, look at it, then throw it over her shoulder.

Her eyes darted frantically from piece to piece through the scattered mail. She knew about the size and shape it

i'm right here

would be, just your standard letter—either that small, personal size or the larger business size, depending on the anger. The problem was it might have slid under some of that brightly colored, glossy junk mail he was now rolling on. There were only several letters there, but his scrunched-up, red face indicated he could pop to his feet any second.

The *whack* slithered back to them—"whack." But he paid no attention to it, rolling around, clutching his arms around his shins, his knees pulled up to his chest. He rolled around in a ball, first on his back, then over to his front, onto his knees, squinting a tight knot of a face. He was still groaning when she sprung to her feet with a letter and then scampered away like a scolded cat. He tried to rise but couldn't, collapsing back onto his knobby knees. "Whack." He breathed hard, sucking in and pushing out, swinging his bag back over his shoulder, crawling out of the several pieces of her mail on the ground.

"I wonder if any of us deserves any of us," he muttered to the sidewalk.

waiting room

You slide down shiny summer days, slippery and clean, like glass. You slide down them while I sit in a shoe box of a waiting room—a cell of tight, cold, stiff, plain school walls and insane tile floors and bland, arithmetic-gray hospital ceiling tiles—a glove box, a mail box, a filing cabinet, a gray metal desk—wounds that remind me of her.

The old lamp hurts me. The floor. The ashtray. The light switch. I have no more magic words to heal them. There is nothing left to say to them.

I'm sitting on an old green couch between a fat guy with a gunshot wound and a tiny teenage girl suffering from anorexia. He took the shot while hunting. She is pale—barely a girl, barely there, barely anything. Her shyness wedges her deep into the couch, pounding her into a tight knot.

They say she's thinking of leaving town, that she's out there in it—swimming the streets, taking the leaves and clouds for a walk, showing up the wind, tempting it, showing it how it's done, staring right down its throat.

And I already feel her slipping away. I already hear her shadow haunting me. She'll leave it lying here like an old

i'm right here

rug. It will stand seriously at my bed as I sleep. It'll stand tall and cold. Little by little it'll wake me by quietly whispering in my ear as it blends into the morning's indigo darkness.

It'll whisper places we shared. It'll whisper neighborhoods and apartments and buildings and businesses. Invisibly these used bookstores, secondhand shops, and coffee houses will slowly wake me.

You know I'll try to find her, in my spare time, like a hobby, and it'll drag behind me. It'll mope and shuffle down the sidewalks of my life, living these halls, wandering every street at once, looking for us.

The wind follows her, pulling the clouds and the trees and uprooting other shadows—shadows of buildings and lives, pulling them out of town with her, pulling the sky and places and events.

And although these places are, in a sense, still here, I feel them slipping away as well. I feel my entire life slipping away, everything warm and familiar is being pulled away. And here I am, just sitting still—wondering what she's doing now, waiting for my life to begin again.

The man with the gunshot is empty-room quiet, barebulb pale, rainy-day sweating, back-of-the-bus sad. He's plywood rough; the girl is simple, covered in acne. Neither really cares for much of anything. But how did they happen upon such a system of beliefs?

They're paging through magazines from a stack on the floor. He's slowly flipping through a hunting publication. She's staring down into a fashion periodical. Watching them slowly turn each page convinces me not to investigate that stack.

He holds his side as he pages. His arm holding the magazine is wrapped tightly around his large belly where he took the blow. He holds his belly with a pale, concerned look on his face, trying to hold everything in. Suddenly he nudges me and pulls a couple of gunshot wounds from his jacket pocket. He hands me one and nods. I work it in my hands. It's hard and stiff, like an old cheap plastic plate of hers, and she strolls down her life, dragging that soggy wind and orange sky of hers, reflected before me in my hands.

two lovers entangled in an unspeakable mess

His suit was a weird green, a golden olive in the sun; her thin black dress a dangling dark hole.

"He must have loved you dearly," he said sipping his tea.

"I'm not so sure," she said looking down into her tiny hands, woven together on the table. She sat straight and still, crisply folded in her chair. He was hunched over in his chair, sideways as usual.

dangle me up the river pajama man

"I shouldn't pick up girls like you like this . . ." he said, lying on his back, limply dangling his head backward over the side of the mattress. "I'm pretty drunk."

"That doesn't matter," she said, sitting up with her hands cupped in her lap. Their legs were entangled, the room was a complete mess.

1923

*(they found him in a ditch at the edge of town,
that really great weekend/smile on his face)*

All Grandpa ever told us was how he had to walk the whole way back after he woke up—or came to, really—lying in his soaked underwear that Monday morning in the tall, damp weeds of a marsh about five miles from town. He never talks about that scar either. He just smiles as he looks into it, the way you'd look at a baby as it totters, taking its first, careful little steps.

hullabaloo

January fourteenth. The doorbell rang. This was quite unusual for the time of night, 7:20. My plump wife, Borgadora, was sandblasting the dishes in the basement while I relaxed with my evening paper on a cold cinder block in my favorite spot, a damp, uncomfortable corner of the living room. Our living room, a bland nothingness; a bleak suburban landscape; monotonous, uniform, absent of identity in its conformity: an interchangeable postcard sent from a relative, or better still, a painting bought on the side of the road and given by a relative as a gift. The doorbell rang again. Quite odd, I thought.

"Get that," reminded my sluggish wife in dark cliche´ minimalism, a crippling blow.

"Hmmm," I mumbled as I gruntingly forced myself out of the cinder block. I folded the paper and set it on my favorite brick, then started for the door; around the pastel green guillotine, tiptoeing through the land mines, performing a high-stepping jig through the barbed wire. I watched my steps carefully, looking down at my dancing feet so as not to step on any of the thin, rusty nails protruding from the floor, the sharply pointed intruder-proof peacekeepers. I turned

i'm right here

on the spotlights and swung open the heavy steel and ten-inch concrete door. Outside, standing on our steps was a tiny man in red overalls, casting a tiny shadow. This was very surprising, I thought.

"Cut it out!" shouted the little man in a snotty, whiny, sophisticated voice. "Or else!" He pulled a tiny flamethrower from behind his back and waved it boastfully in the cold night air. He then turned, hopped off the steps and trotted down the walk.

At the curb was an old red tow truck, and beside the rusty tow truck stood a seven foot tall giant dressed in a leather tunic. The giant had very long, scraggly hair. He smiled and waved politely at me.

"Who is it?" said my wife, attacking in her typical way.

"Nobody," I retaliated in my standard, middle-aged, middle-class American fashion.

The battle began.

"What's it like out?" blitzed my wife samely from her basement bunker. This was a particularly effective weapon, especially if she rattled a few dishes afterward.

She did.

"Oh, not too bad," I charged blandly, ordinarily, non-committally. This was a great submission response. I thought for sure I could break her with it. I thought for sure it would force her into a fit. It would cause her to throw down her dishrags and propane equipment, run in here and complain about how she's been doing the dishes and vacuuming and other work for the past nineteen years and all. I thought for sure it would cause her to say something of worth and value. It would cause her to think, to talk, to express, to show her true feelings.

"What's on TV tonight?"

hullabaloo

Damn. I didn't break her. Well, she won't break me. I fired off a quick "Nothing much," then watched the tiny man disappear into that old red tow truck.
I closed and bolted the heavy door.
The silence that radiated from the basement was broken only periodically by a few dishes rattling.
What a brutally clever weapon, I thought.
She's not going to crack me, I reassured myself. No way.
More rattling.
That's it, that's enough, I've had it. No, wait. Better calm down. I'm not going to give in. I almost lost, I almost showed emotion. I know, I'll get her with some more paper shaking, maybe not shower for a few days again.

I turned from the door to return to my cinder block, where I had spent each night the past ten years after returning home from my bland job. Then a thought of that little man flashed through my chalkboard brain. That little man—how odd an experience, I thought, as I made my way through the olive drab living room. I had heard about such random events, crazy people randomly shouting at people or tying shopping carts to the backs of cars at supermarkets or cutting down every tree in someone's yard. That tiny man . . . Quite odd, I thought.

I stood silently for a moment by a stack of my wife's old magazines. She's such a nostalgic, paging through them on Tuesday nights. "Remember this, Honey? Remember this?" she says pointing to the pictures of pasty-faced presidents and dark, chalky coal-mine disasters and blindingly bright jumbo jet plane crashes; fiery blooming, unfolding petals of orange and yellow technology. She pages through them proudly, adoringly, like photo albums. These people, places, and events have become our loving children. They write us weekly, and we visit them when we can. That flood in

i'm right here

Kampuchea, that twelve-car pileup near Cleveland, that cosmetic surgery scam in Gainesville.

    I was returning to my cinder block, but found myself walking into the kitchen. I heard my wife stomping up the basement stairs similarly. We met in the kitchen. I said, "Borgadora, what's happened to you? You used to be so beautiful, and now you're nothing but a giant bossy nothing!"

    My wife responded by saying, "What has happened to me? What has happened to you?! We used to be so beautiful, and now *you're* nothing but a big lazy nothing, you never want to do anything anymore. Oh, we were so beautiful! Now you're just like that little mechanic who peeked his head in through the basement window and waved that haunting acetylene equipment in my face—"

    "I just saw that tiny man," I interrupted excitedly. "He was just at the door!" I pointed. "And threatened me with that same blowtorch-like equipment!"

    My wife covered her face with her hands. "Why must I be haunted by the way things once were!" she cried.

    I felt awful, seeing my wife unhappy this way. I thought it would only last a moment, but she just stood there, quivering. I was trying to think of something that would make her happy, hoping it wasn't too late, but not coming through with anything as my head was a lifeless wasteland, barren of any vegetation whatsoever. But then that tiny man wandered into my mind. My mind was a living room, with curtains drawn from the world. The chairs were empty there, and the furniture plain, but the television was on and my wife and I sat watching the television, watching this man in this room from our living room. The man began to dance about crazily, faster and faster. He turned on his little flamethrower and did away with the room. The curtains burned away and the bright midnight moon shone in. The room smelled of gas.

My mind smelled of gas and I reached over and pulled out the silverware drawer and held it in front of my wife. The silverware jingled as I shook the drawer from side to side. My wife peeked her face through her hands and smiled, and I said, "Hey, let's make some sculptures like the old days when we would go down to the rail yard and have romantic bean dinners by the light of a campfire, and we would bring home all that beautiful scrap metal lying about and you would fuse it into that magical art of yours and you would add whatever hubcaps or license plates we could find on the way home. Sometimes we would sit for hours, the house stinking of that wonderfully tangy gas from your equipment." My voice hummed as tenderly as the years would allow. "Let's get out that old equipment of yours—I'm certain it's around somewhere." I rattled the drawer again. "I'll model for you."

"You always did enjoy that, didn't you. Sitting nude while I wore my smock and heavy gloves. But dear, I'm not as young as I used to be."

"Hey, listen, the Hendersons just got a new lawn mower. I bet that would pose a real challenge."

"Oh, I'm pretty rusty I'm sure."

I began to unbutton my shirt. I handed my wife the silverware drawer and finished taking off my shirt, then I removed my undershirt and unzipped my trousers. I walked out to the living room, pulling my legs from my pants as I hopped, my pasty belly glowing a pale white, like the moon. "Listen," I said excitedly, "you dig out your equipment just like the old days, and I'll be right back with the Henderson's new mower." I stood in the doorway, bending at the waist to remove my underclothing. As I straightened, I noticed my wife beaming at me from the kitchen.

I turned and snuck into the grass, the dew forcing my socks to cling to my feet as I raced to the neighbor's garage.